MORE THAN THIS

ANA JOLENE

MORE THAN THIS
MOONRISE BEACH SERIES, BOOK THREE
Copyright © 2018 Ana Jolene

This book is a work of fiction. The characters, events, and places portrayed in this book are products of the author's imagination and are either fictitious or are used fictitiously. Any similarity to real persons, living or dead, is purely coincidental and not intended by the author.

Cover Design by Arie Bea
Formatting: Champagne Book Design

ISBN: 978-1-9994032-0-1

For Dad
I am always grateful

A NOTE TO READERS

Hunter Happa-Hewitt completely stole my heart when he first walked onto the page. His strength and courage was so inspiring and so, I knew I had to pair him up with someone just as fierce as he was. Sam Cosi isn't your typical heroine, but I hope you love her tough girl personality as well as her charms. Although this book marks the end of the Happa-Hewitt sibling stories, you will see more of them in the rest of the Moonrise Beach series. And if you haven't already, don't forget to check out Dacey and Greyson's love story in CLOSE TO YOU, the first book of the Moonrise Beach series as well as Hutch and Maison's story in SWEET AS SIN. Each book is written to stand alone but they will be part of a larger series for your enjoyment.

If you enjoy this book, please sign up for my newsletter so you don't miss out on any future Moonrise Beach releases on my website: www.anajolene.com. And if you like darker, more grittier stories, my New Adult Dystopian series, Glory MC, might be the thing for you! There are several books already available in the series (GLORY, ORIGIN, and NIRVANA) with plans for more to come this year!

Happy Reading!
—Ana

ONE

I T WAS NEARLY TIME TO CALL IT A DAY WHEN SAMANTHA Cosi picked up her phone and explained the events she'd just witnessed to her latest client. "Yes," she reiterated. "He met a blonde woman at a motel during his lunch. They stayed in the room for about an hour."

Even though she was the only one in her office, Sam kept her voice soft and sympathetic, knowing that her words were no doubt going to ruin her client's life.

Mrs. Donna Westfield had hired her a couple of days ago to follow her husband around. Apparently he'd been acting strange lately and she wanted to know what was going on with him. This kind of job was typical of her. As one of the most common reasons why clients sought out a private investigator in the first place, Sam didn't even blink an eye at what she'd discovered. Affairs were as prevalent as cell phones these days; it seemed that everyone had one.

To Sam's surprise though, Mrs. Westfield didn't get upset like most of the other women when they got confirmation that they were being cheated on. In fact, Donna seemed absolutely fine. "Thanks for letting me know, Ms. Cosi," she said in the same tone as if she'd just told her her car was ready to be picked up at the garage. "I'm going to talk to him about it tonight."

"Please. I told you already to call me Sam." She hated being called by her full name. It reminded her too much of her mother. "And you're not going to divorce him?" She couldn't disguise the note of surprise in her voice.

"I want to see what he has to say first."

Wow, that was very . . . reasonable of her. By now, other women would be in hysterics. Sam smirked. When Donna Westfield had walked through her door, Sam had a feeling that she wasn't like most women. She'd been momentarily disappointed that her case had been just like any one of her regulars. However, the way Donna was handling all this made her once again think that this woman was different.

Normally, Sam hated having to console her clients. She knew she didn't have to, but when a woman's world was falling apart because of what she'd told them, Sam always felt a bit of remorse. But she didn't have to do that with Donna. The woman seemed like she could go on with her life without her husband and be perfectly content.

Now if only more of women's thinking was like hers.

"Okay, then."

"Thanks for everything you've done, Sam," Mrs. Westfield said. "I'll make sure you're paid by morning."

"Thank you." She had this month's rent due next week and this would lighten the hit a little bit. After hanging up, Sam yawned and stretched, noting that she had no other jobs for the day. For once she was free to just go home for the day and relax. Maybe she would have a soak in the tub. After all that she'd seen today, hell, she deserved it.

Just as she started gathering her things to leave, her phone rang. "Dammit." *Of course something like this would happen. When could she ever catch a break?* "Hello?" she said when she picked up the phone. "Cosi Investigations. This is Sam speaking."

"Samantha, how'd the date go?"

Sam barely suppressed her groan. "Mom, I told you to stop calling me that."

"What? Stop calling you by your real name? Don't be ridiculous."

"No one else calls me Samantha. Only you."

"I'm your *mother*," Rosanna said, "and I'm going to call you the name I gave to you when you were born. Now don't avoid the question. How was the date?"

"No sparks," she lied. Well, that wasn't exactly a lie since she had absolutely no feelings for the man her mother was trying to set her up with.

"Really?" Rosanna sounded devastated. "I really thought you two would hit it off."

"Yup. Sorry."

"No need to apologize. Sometimes love takes a little more work. Don't worry, I'll find you someone before the wedding."

"Mom, it's *fine*. I don't need a date for the wedding!"

"Yes, you do," she insisted. "Your sister is already getting married before you and if you're not going to be walking down the aisle soon, you should at least have a date to the wedding."

Ugh! Why did mothers have to be so annoying all the time? She was only thirty-one years old and she wasn't in a rush to be the bimbo bride to some lowlife loser who couldn't even tell the truth about his job!

The man that her mother had been trying to set her up with had been a total phony. He claimed to be a successful real estate agent but after a quick background check on the guy, Sam found out that it was actually *his uncle* who was the real estate agent and he was just helping him out. After discovering the scumbag's lies, she didn't even bother showing up to their date. If the guy couldn't be honest about his job, what else would he lie about?

"I'll find someone else for you," Rosanna vowed.

"Mom—"

"Let's just make sure that the rest of Serena's wedding is perfect and that bitch, Alyssa, doesn't ruin everything."

Sam had to smile at her mother's sudden change in tone. Alyssa was everyone's pain in the ass. She was Serena's fiancé's ex and she was batshit crazy. When she'd found out about her ex-boyfriend's engagement to her sister, she'd flipped out, appearing at their house and threatening Aaron and her sister. Sam had been there at the time to witness it all and called it in, and although the police had taken Alyssa away, that didn't stop her from harassing them through phone calls and emails. Sam had no respect for women like that. Why were they so desperate to be loved by someone who didn't care for them anymore? Didn't they have more self-worth for themselves? At least she was sure that she wouldn't be throwing herself at just any man who leered at her.

"Don't worry, Mom. I've got it covered. Serena's wedding will be amazing."

She felt bad for lying. Although she meant it when she said that she wouldn't allow Alyssa to ruin Serena's wedding, there was also the fact that Sam hated weddings and she would no doubt be dreading every moment leading up to the big day no matter how much she loved her little sister.

If it was up to her, she'd fly solo for the night, but her mother was adamant about not allowing her eldest daughter to show up without a man on her arm. And therein lay the crux of her trouble.

The sudden rap on her door pulled her out of her personal dilemma. Sam turned to the door and caught sight of a large shadow. "Mom, I have to go. Someone is here."

"At this hour? Aren't you going to go home soon?"

"Yes, I will," she bit off. "Right after I see what this guy wants." She wasn't expecting anyone to come by but when the man knocked again, it was clear that he seemed impatient. After a promise to call her mother back later, Sam hung up and opened the door. "Can I help you?"

She thought it might be a father looking to do another background check on his daughter's boyfriend or something, but she couldn't quite hide her shock at seeing Hunter Happa-Hewitt before her. "Wh—what are you doing here?"

Her best friend's older brother smiled down at her. "Leaving for the day already?"

"Ah, yeah. I was on my way out." Sam shot him what she hoped was a friendly smile. For whatever reason, Hunter's presence always seemed to throw her a little off-kilter. "Just so you know, Hutch isn't here."

"I'm not looking for Hutch."

Huh? If he wasn't here for his brother, then what the hell was he doing here? She took that moment to take him in. She'd already noticed his broad shoulders through the door. And with his height, she could believe all the great things Hutch had told her about his brother during his football glory days.

She felt downright puny standing next to him and she wasn't a particularly small woman to begin with. At six feet, Sam often stood head to head with a lot of her male friends, including Hutch. But Hunter had to have at least two more inches on her. Combined with the breadth of his chest and shoulders, the unyielding strength of his body was obvious.

To put it in simpler terms, the man was walking, talking sex appeal. But what was he doing here?

She was by no means on friendly terms with her best friend's brother. Despite his casual uniform of a white T-shirt and jeans, Hunter looked on edge. That still didn't explain his presence. Why was he here? "If you're not here looking for Hutch, then why are you here?"

A stiff smile flashed over his lips before he settled down in one of the seats beside her desk. "You're always so straightforward. I like that."

"I prefer things that way. It cuts through the bullshit."

He smiled wider now and Sam felt herself stiffen. Dammit, that smile of his always did something strange to her, but she wasn't going to reveal how it made her head feel light. "I won't waste more of your time, but I wanted to talk to you about the accident . . ."

Sam braced herself for the worst. His father, Matthew Hewitt, had recently gotten into a car accident. When they'd learned the news, he and Hutch's fiancée, Maison, had come to her house looking for Hutch so that they could all go to the hospital together. Sam had gone with them, wanting to be there for her best friend.

That was also the time when she'd spent time with Hunter's son, Owen. The rowdy five-year-old had been confused about what was happening still and with everyone's emotions at an all-time high, Sam had pulled him away to spend time with him while the Happa-Hewitts dealt with everything else. Although Sam never considered herself good with children, she had enjoyed spending time with Owen. Unfortunately, she couldn't say the same thing with the kid's father.

Despite being Hutch's best friend for years, Sam had limited interaction with his older brother. She'd tended to stay away from Hutch's family mainly because she believed they still blamed her for convincing Hutch to join the Army with her. Although she hadn't made the cut, Hutch had, and he'd spent years serving while she'd returned to Moonrise Beach to try and rebuild her life here.

But having limited exposure to the Happa-Hewitts didn't mean that she didn't care about them. After years of Hutch telling her stories about his family, Sam felt like she knew them well, which made Matthew's accident harder to bear.

"How is he doing?" she asked. The last time she'd asked Hutch about him, he'd still been unconscious.

"He's doing better I think."

"That's good." They'd been all so worried.

Hunter suddenly looked up and pinned her with a dark gaze. "I know we don't know each other well or anything like that, but I need your help."

Her help? Why would Hunter need her help? Concern filled her as Hunter swallowed thickly. "What's going on?" If his father was doing better, then what was he so worried about?

This late in the day Hunter had a sexy shadow lining his jaw and his incendiary eyes looked even more compelling as his jaw tightened. He looked like he suddenly wasn't sure, and Sam's investigative alarms started to go off in her head. "I don't think what happened to my father was an accident," Hunter said in a low, hushed tone.

"What? What makes you think it was something else?" She needed a moment to process this. *Just what exactly was Hunter insinuating?* "I thought they said he crashed into a tree." It'd been raining all day and Hutch had come to see her after he'd tried—and failed—to see Maison.

"He did," Hunter confirmed. "But I feel like there's something else going on."

"Like what?" He couldn't be implying what she thought he was . . .

But then he said the words she wished he hadn't. "Like maybe someone tried to kill him."

Sam felt her stomach bottom out. No. *No way.* Who would want to kill Matthew Hewitt? "What makes you think that?" Her voice came out sharp and unrestrained.

"When he came to yesterday, his first words to me were about his business partner."

Wait. He'd been awake? How come Hutch hadn't mentioned this to her? Now Sam's head was reeling. "What did he say?"

"He told me not to let Clive take his place at Gleam."

"Huh? Why would he say that?"

Hunter shook his head. "I don't know. Maybe he's the one who—"

Sam shot her hands up. "Whoa, okay. Before we start jumping to conclusions, I have to ask, have you talked to the cops about this already?" *Why come to her with this information?*

Hunter shook his head again. "No. Not yet. I want you to do some digging first."

Sam couldn't hide her shock. "Wait. You want to *hire* me?"

When Hunter nodded, Sam put her hands up. "Whoa, I'm not sure I can do this."

"Why not?" Hunter suddenly stood, and although he wasn't trying to intimidate her, his size and the way he towered over her had the same effect.

Sam had to stand her ground. "This isn't the kind of stuff that I do." Background checks were more her thing. While she did help Deacon Thorpe of the Moonrise Beach Police Department from time to time, she wasn't a cop and something like this definitely required some police involvement. "What other evidence do you have to support all this?"

"I don't have much to be honest," he admitted. "That's why I'm hoping you can look into his business partner for me. Although I've known Clive for a while, we don't have much contact with one another apart from the occasional event."

"You want me to investigate Clive Davenport?" She

couldn't believe this! Sam shook her head. "I'm not sure I can do this." She was normally game for anything, but even this sounded like extra trouble she didn't need. She already had her mother and her sister's wedding to worry about without throwing this case into the mix.

To her surprise, Hunter leaned forward, his incendiary eyes turning pleading in an instant. He looked so tired that she wondered how much sleep he'd gotten since the last time she saw him. "I think you should talk to the police," she said softly. If anything he said was true, they'd be able to help him better than she could.

"But I want you to do it."

"What do I have that they don't?" Here, she only had herself to rely on whereas the police department would have specially trained officers and investigators who could achieve better results than she could on her own.

"You're smart. I know you'll be thorough." Hunter paused before saying, "It'll give me some peace of mind."

Sam felt torn between wanting to help and telling him to fuck off. But could she do that to her best friend's brother? Especially after everything that had happened already.

"Are you even sure your father even said those things about Clive?" Why would the CEO of the company say that about his own business partner? What the hell was going on at Gleam?

The corner of Hunter's divine mouth tipped up, making his face look ruggedly handsome. "Are you calling me a liar?" He said it with such a cool, dark resonance that it took her by surprise.

She didn't expect this change in demeanor from him. Just a second ago, he looked so torn up that she almost wanted to pull him into her arms and hold him. *Almost.* But Sam knew better than to act on her impulses. "I'm just saying your eyes look bloodshot and you look like you're about to keel over at any minute. When was the last time you had some decent shut-eye?"

The frown returned. "Not since before the accident."

Jesus. "That's not healthy."

"And that is?" He pointed to the half-empty bottle of whisky she kept behind her desk. A glass sat next to it, ready to be used.

Despite their grim topic of discussion, Sam laughed. "Guess I'm not one to talk, huh?"

With a strained smile, Hunter turned for the door. "I've got no room to judge." He paused to look over his shoulder at her. "Think about it, okay? I know it's a little out there, but I feel like I can trust you better than anyone else at the moment."

"And why is that?" He barely knew her.

Hunter shrugged. "I guess it's because of Hutch. He always runs to you when he's at his lowest. It tells me he trusts you." While that used to be the case, he now had Maison to turn to. Sam doubted she'd be spending that much time with Hutch now.

Her look must've been skeptical because Hunter smiled, hitting her right in the gut. God, what was it about this guy's smile that made her stomach do somersaults? "If you won't do it for me, then do it for Hutch. If there really is something going on, I want to know I took every measure to protect my family."

Sam sighed. *Dammit. How could she argue with that?* She knew the guy wasn't just thinking of his father, but likely his son as well. What if Owen had been in the car with Matthew when the accident had occurred? She felt her stomach clench with fear.

"I'll think about it," she said despite the uncertainty she

felt. She still wasn't sure if she could do this, but Hunter was her best friend's brother. If she turned him away, what would it do to her friendship with Hutch?

"Thank you. I appreciate you talking with me today." With a parting nod, Hunter closed the office door behind him. But even alone in her office, Sam could still smell his scent of expensive forest.

TWO

EARLY THE NEXT MORNING, HUNTER HAPPA-HEWITT made his way back to the hospital with his kid in tow. Unfortunately, this had become their routine as of late. But the idea of having his father sleeping alone in a cold hospital room didn't sit well with him so Hunter always made the extra effort to be there first thing in the morning.

Once again, Owen had fallen back asleep as soon as he'd buckled him in the car and he felt a pang of guilt as he popped him free again and carried him inside.

Despite the time, there were already a lot of people hustling about. Guess 5 a.m. wasn't all that early for some people. Doctors and nurses greeted him as he signed in. A lot of them already knew who he was and made the extra effort to be nice to him because of who his father was. In some worlds, Matthew Hewitt was considered a celebrity.

Hunter felt a lot sturdier than he'd been the last few days as he carried Owen to his father's room. He'd taken Sam's advice and went home to catch some sleep after seeing her. It was a wonder what a full eight hours of sleep did to a person. He was no longer fighting to keep his eyes open and his body felt miraculously healed of its aches and pains, but he still had no idea if she'd accept his offer. He knew he'd surprised her with his visit, but he was getting desperate. Ever since his father had woken up and warned him about Clive, he'd been on edge. Sam might think him paranoid but better that than sorry. And after becoming a father, Hunter had learned how important it was to take precautions, especially when it came to those he cared about.

As he entered the room, he was surprised to find the rest of his family already there. Hutch was staring down at their father by the foot of the bed, hands stuffed into the front pocket of his black jeans. His expression was unreadable as he stared down at their father.

His sister, Dacey, sat by the side of the bed, hand coiled tightly around their father's. He could see every line of worry in her pretty little face as he approached. "Good morning," he greeted as he set Owen down. "Has he woken up yet?"

Dacey shook her head and frowned. "No. Are you sure he woke up last night?"

"I wouldn't lie to you."

Dacey sighed. "Sorry. I didn't mean for it to come out that way. It's just that we've been here for a while already and he hasn't moved at all." After Matthew had come to last night, he'd given his siblings a call. They'd all rushed to see him, but their father hadn't stirred again. Hunter hadn't told them about what their father had said, deciding that it was better to keep this to himself for the time being. He still wasn't sure if what his father had said was real or if it was only just some blabber in a confused state. He also wasn't sure what his siblings would do if they found out, so he was keeping his mouth shut until he could figure out a plan of action.

"Don't worry." He pulled his sister in his arms and hugged her. "He'll wake up again." Dacey shot him a skeptical look, but she did eventually smile at him. Hunter turned to Hutch. "You okay, man?"

His brother smiled at him, but it didn't quite meet his eyes. He was the one he had to watch out for. Hunter was still getting used to having him around again. And after his stint in the

Army that had Hutch losing half of his lower leg, his brother had changed. He wasn't sure how well he was readjusting to civilian life, but this entire situation probably wasn't helping.

"I'm fine. How about you?"

Hunter shrugged, not wanting to let his brother know that he was actually scared shitless. As the eldest of his siblings, he felt a certain sense of responsibility to take care of all of them. "I could do with some coffee. Do you want some?"

"Thanks, but no, thanks. I already had some."

"Okay, I'm going to grab one for myself then. Can you watch Owen for me?"

"Sure." Hutch immediately turned to Owen, pulled him into his arms. Hunter smiled. He never expected to have his family all together once again, so he guessed he should be thankful they were all here despite the circumstances.

"I'll be right back," he said before heading for the café. As he walked down the hallway Hunter was surprised to see Sam walking through the hospital doors. Because of her height, she stood out. But it was also because she was yelling at one of the nurses who was refusing her admittance. "Hey, what are you doing here?"

She snapped her head in his direction, eyes widening. "Thank God. I've been looking for you!" Her cheeks were flushed from arguing with the other woman and although her hair was pulled back into a high ponytail, several strands had fallen free, dangling around her face prettily.

Sam shot a sneer at the other woman and turned her back on her. "You didn't give me a way to contact you and I didn't want to ask Hutch for your number because I'm not actually sure that I can do this for you."

Hunter felt his smile falter. "Why not?" In seeing her here, he thought that she was going to take on the job.

"I'm sorry but it's just not the kind of stuff I do."

"Come on, I need you." And if he had to beg, he would.

Sam shook her head, sending more tendrils free from her ponytail. "I'm sorry but the answer is no."

Dammit. What was he going to do now?

The hospital doors opened again, and to both their surprise Deacon Thorpe walked in. As the police detective caught sight of him, he walked straight over to them. "Hey, Deacon," Sam greeted. Hunter wasn't surprised that they already knew each other. It seemed that everyone in Moonrise Beach did.

"Good morning, Sam." Deacon flashed a smile at her before turning back to him. "Hey, can I talk to you for a moment?"

Getting the message, Sam stepped away to give them both some privacy. Shit. He wasn't ready for her to leave yet. He wanted to talk to her some more and maybe convince her—

Deacon leaned in, his eyes conveying more concern than he was comfortable with. "So we've discovered something about the car," he started.

Hunter felt his chest tighten. Oh God, he was almost afraid to ask. Was what his father said true? Could it not have been an accident at all? "What is it?"

"Looks like someone tampered with the brakes on your father's car. Might've been why he lost control."

Holy shit. He dropped his head in his hands and, thankfully, Deacon just gave him a moment to compose himself. He felt like his very bones were shaking. Fear put him in a stronghold that he struggled for breath.

This was so fucked up. Would they have found something earlier if they thought that this was something more than a simple car accident? Why hadn't anyone noticed anything before now?

He lifted his head to ask just that when he caught sight of

Sam walking back to him. She glanced between them, concern marring her features. "Is everything okay here?"

"Everything is not okay." He didn't want to admit it before until Matthew was out of the danger zone but it would seem that it would be a while until he could consider his family safe again.

Sam rested a gentle hand on his arm. "Hey, come on. Tell me what's going on. Maybe I can help."

Deacon looked surprised by Sam's sudden concern. When he cut a glance at him and he nodded, he filled her in on the details. "Oh my God," Sam breathed as he finished. "That's terrible." Was she thinking of their conversation last night again? Would she help him now?

He was surprised to see the amount of worry in her gaze. She may not be part of his family, but she clearly cared about Matthew. How much had Hutch actually told her about them?

Deacon's words cut through his thoughts. "I'm really sorry about all this. We're launching an investigation to find out what really happened. But I thought I'd let you know first. Do you want me to tell the rest of your family too?"

"No, no. It's fine. I'll do that." He was already dreading it, but he wanted to be the one to tell his family the news. He'd hoped to keep this hidden for at least a few more days, but if the police were going to launch an investigation like Deacon said, there was no way he could keep it from his family any longer. With his father's status, this would be something reporters would quickly jump on.

Deacon nodded. "Okay. I really am sorry, man. I promise you we'll do everything in our power to find out who did this."

"Thanks, man." After quickly hugging his friend, Hunter turned back to Sam. She was still watching him with those lovely emerald eyes. "You have to help me."

Her eyes widened at his demand. "What do you want me to do?"

"You already know."

"Hunter, you have the cops already on it. What good am I going to do?"

"Plenty. You're an excellent private investigator and I'll pay you good money for your time." If someone out there wanted his father dead, then he was going to do everything in his power to stop that person. "Besides, you're the only person I trust with this."

"You hardly know me!"

"You took care of my kid." And though he hadn't told anyone about it, Owen had had such a great time with Sam that he couldn't stop talking about her.

Sam shook her head. "Anyone who wasn't sick in the head would've done that."

Not everyone. To be honest, he hadn't expected it from someone like her. Sam Cosi didn't look like the nurturing type, but she'd been so gentle with his kid that she had besotted Owen. And when he'd asked when they were going to see her again, Hunter had told him that he didn't know. Owen wasn't the only one who was disappointed in the answer. He was too.

Sam Cosi wasn't like any other woman he'd met. And she certainly wasn't like anyone he'd ever dated. She was tough and independent, running into trouble where other women seemed to flee from it. If there was anyone who could figure this out, it was Sam.

His voice lowered as he leaned into her. "Come on. I need you to do this for me."

"I can't. It's not my area of expertise."

"Bullshit. You're more than capable of something like this."

Her huff of laughter had him smiling. "Flattering me will

get you nowhere."

"No?" But she was smiling at him now. That was progress to him. "Please, Sam. Do it for Hutch." He knew he was playing into her friendship with his brother, but he didn't think Hutch would mind. As much as they'd fought, he believed his siblings really did care about each other.

He could see Sam debating with herself. He knew what he was asking was too much, but he was hoping, praying that behind that lean, hard muscle and tough skin, was a soft center.

"Fine, I'll do it."

Hunter let out a breath of relief. "Great."

"But only because I'm worried too," Sam added. "Something about all this is strange to me. What did your father say to you again?"

"He said don't let Clive take over his place at Gleam."

Sam blew out a breath. "Yeah, if that doesn't give you the creepy-crawly feelings, then I don't know what else will."

"Yeah, tell me about it." He'd been so shocked by the words that he'd probably sat there for a few minutes completely motionless.

"Okay, I'm going to check in on this Clive guy," Sam said.

"Thank you. I've known him for a long time so I can't see him as anything other than the good friend he was to my father, but something isn't right." He shook his head. "To think he might be behind all this . . ."

"Give me your number so I can call you if I find something." When Sam pulled out her phone, he recited his digits. "Great. Thanks," she said as she put her phone back away. "I'll be in touch soon."

"I'll come by your office later this week to pay you." He'd likely need to be with his family for a little bit once he broke the news to them.

But Sam shook her head. "No need. I'm not going to ac-cept payment for this."

"Huh? Why not?"

"I'm not going to accept money from you. Like I said, this isn't my usual MO so I'd prefer the police handle this, but I may be able to help along the way."

"Are you sure?" He wasn't lacking in money. He could pay her a hefty sum for her efforts.

Sam gave a curt nod. "I'm sure. Hutch is my best friend and if he needs my help, then I'll do whatever I can to make sure he and his family are safe."

"Thank you," he breathed. He was really glad to hear that.

With a smile, Sam turned for the doors and Hunter watched her until she disappeared into her car. His anxiety had lessened now that she'd agreed to help them, but he knew bet-ter than to think everything was going to be okay now.

He'd thought that with his father waking up, things would get easier for them, but so far, it was only getting worse. If Matthew woke up again, what else would they discover about that rainy night?

Shaking his head, Hunter turned back, his coffee totally forgotten from his mind.

THREE

THE FIRST THING THAT SAM DID WAS HEAD BACK TO her office. A new case meant that she had to start at the beginning. Even though she refused to accept payment for this, she was going to treat this with the same level of commitment and seriousness as she did with all her other cases.

While she'd gone to the hospital with the intention to tell Hunter no, it had taken her a long time to decide that. She'd lain in bed thinking about his incendiary eyes but knew this was better off to be dealt with by the police. So why then had she agreed to it today? With him standing so close, the rich leather and sandalwood scent of him filling her nostrils, she probably would've said yes to anything he asked of her.

But it was more than her attraction to him. She hated seeing Hunter hurting and she knew she wouldn't mind checking things out for the Happa-Hewitts. It also helped that it was Deacon who was going to be leading this investigation, someone she was good friends with and had worked with many times before. If it had been someone else, then she probably wouldn't have been so quick to agree. But now that she had confirmation from Deacon, she worried that something might actually be going on at Gleam Enterprises with Clive.

Although she knew of Matthew Hewitt's business partner, that was pretty much where her knowledge of the man ended. Sam knew she would have to do some research and refresh her memory on the man who supposedly tried to get his business partner killed. "Wow," she muttered to herself. She went from cheating bastards to attempted murderers in a single day. "How the hell do you get yourself in these situations?"

Settling at her desk, the first thing Sam set out to do was a background check. But as she started her work, her mind wandered to Hunter again. What was it about this man that got to her? She'd spent years around Hutch and never felt a stirring of desire or lust for the guy. But simply standing beside his brother was enough to have her make her want to jump him.

She supposed it all had to do with their presence. While Hutch was a skilled warrior on the field, he didn't stir up the fantasies like Hunter did. The man oozed calm control and Sam found that to be an attractive quality in a man. She liked men who weren't easily swayed by other people's opinions and men who clearly had a passion. In this case, she was sure nothing would stand in the way of him finding out what happened to his father. Not even her.

That was why she wasn't going to take the case on in an official capacity. It just didn't feel right to take money from Hutch's brother when she, too, was concerned for Matthew's safety.

He seemed remarkably put together for a man who'd just found out that someone had tried to kill his father. Sam didn't want to test him more though. She was going to help where she could. If Hutch had been the one to come to her, she wouldn't have argued with him at all. So why then would she refuse the same from his brother?

Sam shook her head and focused back on the screen before her. Even if she spent the entire night staring at the screen, it wouldn't tell her what the police wouldn't already know. If she really wanted to find out what happened that night, then she had to know more about Clive *and* Matthew to determine if something looked out of place or suspicious. And the only way she could do that was to go back to the night of the accident.

The shrill sound of her phone ringing startled her. Cursing, Sam realized too late that it was her mother calling. "Samantha, you're in luck! I've found another man for you."

"Mom, this is not a good time. I'm working right now."

"Oh, you got a new case?"

"That's right." She was keeping her responses short to hopefully discourage her mother from asking more questions.

"What's it about?"

Ugh. "Mom, you know I can't share that information."

"But I'm your mother," Rosanna whined.

"Yes, you are. But I still can't tell you." Mostly because she'd try to tell her how to do her job and she already had enough of her telling her how she should live her life.

"Fine, fine. I won't bug you anymore." Sam would've been relieved if not for the fact that her mother said, "So this guy I met is really amazing, Samantha. I think you'll like him."

Sam decided to indulge her. "Let me guess, is he some kind of businessman again?"

There was a gasp on the other end of the line. "How did you know?"

Sam suppressed a smile. "Because I know you and you have a thing for guys in suits." Which was totally not her preference at all. Sam liked her men a little more . . . rougher-looking. Someone not so polished. Someone like Hunter.

"What's wrong with a man in a suit? At least we'll know what he looks like when he comes to the wedding."

Ugh. Here we go again. "I don't even know this guy, Mom." How did she expect her to bring a man she didn't even know to an event as important as her sister's wedding?

"But you will," her mother assured her. "Once you go out

with him a few times."

Sam groaned. "Mom, how many times do I have to tell you, I don't need you to find me a date. If I wanted one, I can find one myself."

"You've had thirty-one years to find yourself a man. All you have to do is meet him."

"Meet him?"

"Yes, I've already set up a date for you. Tonight."

"Tonight? Mom, how could you?"

"What?" she asked innocently.

"You can't just set me up with a random dude I don't know!"

"Why not? People do it all the time on that Internet site. What's it called again? Timber?"

Sam groaned loudly. *Oh no. No.* She was *not* discussing Tinder with her mother. She had to be stern about this or her mother would never stop. "Sorry, Mom, but you have to cancel. I'm not going."

"Don't be ridiculous. What's the worst that can happen?"

"Oh, I don't know. Maybe he's some serial killer or rapist! Have you thought about that?"

"How can you say that about Lorenzo? He's a sweetheart!"

"Lorenzo? What kind of name is *Lorenzo?*"

"It's an honest name. And he's an honest man. Come on, do it for me, darling, just once." *Just once? Just this week her mother had pushed three different guys onto her already!*

"Mom, I really wish you would stop this."

Whether it was her words or her tone when she'd said it but some of the fire had died from her mother's excitement. "Oh, fine. I was just trying to help you. Can you blame a mother for worrying over her own child?"

Damn, now she was the one who felt terrible. *Ugh.* "Okay.

Fine," Sam said. "I'll go."

Rosanna immediately lit up. "Good! I know you won't regret it."

Oh, she would. Sam knew it. But if she wanted a small reprieve from her mother then she had to find a date for the wedding. It didn't matter that she didn't give two shits about whoever this Lorenzo guy was. She just needed someone to be with her on that day. If meeting with this guy would get her mother off her back, then maybe she could focus on her job instead of her pathetic love life.

Her phone beeped, indicating that she'd just received a text. It was from Hutch who said he was heading over and would arrived in just a few minutes. "Sorry, Mom. But I've got to go. I'll call you back."

As promised, Hutch was knocking on her door a few minutes later. "Hey."

"Hey." She hadn't seen him since the day of the accident. She knew things had to be hard for him so she hadn't bugged him to come see her. She was glad for his presence now. "How've you been?"

Hutch drew his hand through his hair. "Things are really fucked up right now."

"I'm really sorry. We all thought it was an accident. To think that someone may have wanted this . . ."

Hutch looked surprised. "You heard already? Did Hunter tell you?"

"I was there when Deacon told Hunter actually."

"You were? But how—"

"I was at the hospital earlier today. Hunter didn't tell you?"

"No, he didn't." Hutch moved to sit in one of the chairs. He slumped down so quickly it was almost like he was a puppet who'd had his strings cut. He looked just as bad as Hunter had been last night when he was low on sleep.

She thought about what Hunter had said to her about Hutch. About how he always ran to her when he was upset about something. She thought that it would stop now that he had Maison in his life but here he was again, seeking her companionship. "Where's Maison?" she asked.

"She's working today. I didn't want her to worry any more than she already is so I told her to go into work today."

Sam nodded. "Gleam needs her." With their CEO out of the game for the moment, they'd need someone as competent as her to see them through.

"So how's work been?" Hutch asked.

"Ah, well." She wasn't sure how much to divulge. Did Hunter tell him that she was going to help with their case? She wanted to respect Hunter, but she would feel bad for lying to her friend. She settled for telling him everything.

"So Hunter wants you looking into Clive?" Hutch asked after she finished explaining everything to him.

"Yes. I've just started my research." She really hoped that he wouldn't mind her involvement, but she really did want to help where she could.

"Good. I hope you find something. I'd like this all to be over with." Impatience rode his tone and Sam felt a pang of sympathy go through her. Throughout their many years of friendship, she'd seen every side of Hutch's character so she was very familiar with the way his emotions worked. It would take a while for Hutch to smile again.

"Don't worry," she said as she turned back to her computer. "I'll work closely with the police to get down to the bottom of this."

"Thanks, Sam." Hutch left a few minutes later, leaving her time to get ready for her date. It mostly consisted of her running a comb through her hair and changing her Chucks for a pair of heels. But that was all Lorenzo was going to get. Besides, she wasn't going to meet him with the intention to impress the guy; she just had to win him over enough to want to hang out with her for a day.

And then she'd be able to go back to what really mattered. To figure out what really happened on that one rainy night.

There were times when Hunter wished he were stronger and tonight was one of those nights. Telling his siblings about what the police had reported had been tough. He thought to protect them by withholding information until he knew exactly what was going on, but he wouldn't be able to hide this. Not when his father was such a well-known man and an investigation like this would no doubt run rampant with the media.

Hunter had just given Owen his dinner and tucked him into his bed. Hutch had returned home only about an hour ago, and although he hadn't mentioned where he'd been, he suspected that he'd gone to see Sam.

He'd seen his own fear glitter in his brother's eyes when he'd shared the news to them and he wondered how much Sam had divulged to him. Would she tell him that he asked her to look into Clive last night?

In addition to his brother, Hunter worried about Dacey too. She was the more sensitive one not just because she was a woman, but she always tended to see the good in people, never expecting any harm or negativity. So when something bad happened, she was always so surprised by it. He used to see it as her being naïve but now he realized it was because Dacey was the glass-half-full kind of person and he could use some of that perspective himself. Just to be safe though, he'd asked Greyson to watch over her.

Now alone, Hunter let out a long groan as he spread out over his mattress. For several moments, he just lay there staring at his ceiling. His life had changed so much. He thought that his divorce with Chrissy had been the worst thing that had happened to him and while it was still up there, he had a feeling that what he was going to do next was going to be a thousand times harder for him. He'd never been the kind of guy to think about the future very much, but when his football career ended, he'd been forced to take a good hard look at himself and figure out what he wanted to do with his life.

At the time, he'd wanted greater stability so he'd proposed to his long-time girlfriend. They'd managed Chrissy's coffeehouse for years during their marriage until their divorce. And now . . . well, and now Hunter was still trying to find his footing.

For nearly all of his adult life, his father had urged him to work at Gleam. Even Dacey had worked there for years before quitting her job to start her own jewelry line. And Hutch had had his round there as well. Out of their entire family, he was the only one who hadn't worked for his father's business.

"Guess it's my turn," he muttered to the ceiling, feeling the oppressive weight of responsibility push him down further into the mattress. Working at Gleam had never been his dream, and until the accident, he'd never intended to follow in his father's footsteps. He'd fought so hard to be something else, but things were rapidly changing and Hunter couldn't just leave his father's company to Clive when he was likely the person responsible for putting his father in the hospital in the first place.

Hunter rolled over and grabbed his phone. He knew what he had to do to make his father happy. And although he had a feeling he might regret this, he didn't want to leave Gleam in the hands of Clive Davenport.

As always, Maison picked up on the first ring. "Hunter?

What's wrong? Is Matthew okay?"

"He's fine," he assured her. Maison was his father's assistant and she tended to worry if not comforted. "But I need your help."

"Of course, what do you need?"

He took a breath before speaking. "I'm going to step into my father's place as CEO of Gleam Enterprises until he fully recovers from the accident." Oh God. He'd really done it and now he couldn't take it back. There was a beat of silence as Maison processed this. "Maison, you still there?"

"Y—yes. We can do that." But she sounded far less sure of herself now. "Are you sure this is what you want to do?" She had to have known that he'd refused his father before.

"Who normally fills in when my father is away?" he asked instead.

"Clive does."

And that was why he had to do this. He had to save Gleam. "Do you think you can make this happen so I can come in tomorrow morning?"

"I can, but it will definitely throw people for a loop."

"This accident threw me for a loop. Look, I'll only stay on until my father returns," he said. "I just want to make sure nothing else happens while he's recovering."

"Of course, sir."

"Good. I guess I'll see you tomorrow?" It came out more as a question and he hated himself for that. Why couldn't he be more like his father who was so sure and confident in himself?

Hunter knew that in doing this, he was going to cause a stir in a lot of people. Gleam Enterprises employed more than 400,000 people but nothing mattered more to him than making sure no one else got hurt with Clive Davenport around. And if that meant getting in harm's way himself, then that was what he was going to do.

"Yes, sir," Maison said. "I'll see you tomorrow."

The next morning, Sam headed for Gleam Enterprises with the intent to get in and get out. She'd wasted enough time yesterday dealing with Lorenzo. Unfortunately, the Italian hadn't been so enamored by her as she expected and had refused her when she'd asked if he'd come to her sister's wedding with her.

He'd flat-out refused her!

Sam would've been offended if she'd actually cared. She was more annoyed by the fact that this douchebag had wasted her evening.

She didn't have time for romance in her life. Most of her life was so fast-paced and unpredictable that most men didn't know how to deal with it. And she wasn't about to waste her own time trying to explain herself to them. She was a working woman and her own boss. What else was there to explain?

News had broken out about Matthew Hewitt and now reporters were outside trying to get some details for their news coverage. Sam groaned as she walked toward the crowd, wishing she could just snap her fingers and make them all disappear. Using her elbows, she pushed her way through the swarm of cameramen and reporters. Why did she agree to work on this case? It was already becoming a pain in her ass and it wasn't even lunchtime yet.

"Excuse me," she said as she slid past several reporters. "I need to get inside." Right as she was about to open one of the doors, her arm was immediately seized and Sam was pulled back. "*Ack!* Watch it!"

She turned to find a big-bear cop holding onto her. "You're not allowed in there, ma'am. Only people working here can go in."

"I *am* working here," she growled, ripping her arm from his grip. She didn't need to say that she didn't actually work *for* Gleam Enterprises but she did have business here.

She scurried in before he could stop her. Now inside, Sam checked to see what floor she needed to take the elevator to before quickly sliding into the cab with the rest of Gleam's workers. By the curious glances shot her way, she knew she stood out like a sore thumb dressed in a pair of dark ripped jeans and a T-shirt while everyone else wore clean-cut office attire. *Hmm, maybe the police officer wasn't wrong to try and stop her.*

Whatever. She would be out of here in no time.

When the doors opened to her floor, Sam stepped out, catching sight of a familiar blonde down the hall. "Hi, Maison," she said when she reached her desk.

Maison looked confused. "Sam? What are you doing here?"

"I came to see you. Do you mind answering a few questions for me?"

The blonde smiled at her, but she could tell that she had her hands full already. She probably should've called in advance or something, but she was already here and she didn't feel like leaving only to come back again.

"How did you even manage to get up here?" Maison asked. "It's a riot out there."

"It was a bit of a struggle but I managed."

Maison's smile widened. "Okay, well, since you're already here, have a seat."

Sam pulled up a chair and settled beside her. "So did Hutch tell you about what happened?"

She was thrilled to see Maison nod because then she wouldn't have to waste time explaining what she did for a living. "You're trying to find out who may have done this to Matthew?"

"That's right."

"Aren't the police doing an investigation already?"

"They are, but I'm specifically looking into Clive Davenport. Is he in today? Do you think I can talk to him?"

"Sorry, he didn't come in today. I think he wanted to avoid the whole media circus."

Dammit. It would've been easier to talk to him here. Now she'd have to try and catch him at his home. "Okay then. Is there any way you can give me a copy of Matthew's schedule? I'd like to know his whereabouts before the accident actually occurred."

"Sure." Maison started typing away at her computer before she turned back to her. "To be honest, I checked it out right after I got news of the accident, but I don't really see anything out of the ordinary." She tilted the computer screen around so that Sam could see it.

"Really?" Sam frowned. "Nothing at all suspicious that may help?"

"Nothing. He wasn't acting weird either. Just his normal, bossy self."

"What about Clive? Has he been acting weird lately?"

Maison shook her head. "No, not at all."

"Well, he was the last person to see him before the accident. I just wonder if something was said that might've caused him to react badly toward Matthew."

"I don't think Clive had anything to do with what happened to Matthew."

She arched a brow at her. "You don't think he's capable of it?"

"No. Not at all." She seemed appalled that she would

suggest such a thing. But why would the cops be looking into Clive if they didn't suspect something was up?

"I don't know much about the man," she admitted. "What can you tell me about him?"

"He's Matthew's best friend. They've known each other for forever. This entire company is built on their friendship."

"That sounds nice." But that wasn't what she wanted to know. She needed the dirt. "What about the employees? Colleagues? What do they think of them?"

"Everyone loves Clive. He's very friendly to everyone, even the cleaners. Matthew, on the other hand"—her voice dropped an octave—"he's a little more private."

"Meaning he doesn't talk to anyone but you."

Maison shot her a small smile. "Of course he does. He just rather I do it most of the time."

Sam laughed. Matthew sounded a whole lot like her. Business first, bullshit *never*. "Okay, so what *aren't* you telling me?" Normally, she wouldn't push too hard. But although Maison may look fragile, she knew she was far from it. Sam figured they could tell it to each other straight.

"Matthew isn't as well-liked in the company as Clive is," Maison revealed. "Like I said, he can be a little bossy and not everyone deals with that as well as I do."

Although Maison may seem shy to most people, Sam realized that she actually wasn't. She just picked her battles better than most people and only spent her time dealing with people who were worth it. If she were smart, she'd take that on too. It might help things with her mother.

"Can you tell me who else would benefit if Matthew died?"

"As far as I know, his money would go to his kids. But Matthew often donated to charity as well." Sam went silent as she processed this. "Oh no. *No*," Maison said at her expression.

"You can't honestly think Hutch had something to do with this! Are you crazy?"

"I didn't say anything."

"No, but you were thinking it!"

"I was *contemplating* it, but I know it's not a real possibility." Hutch was with her the entire time so he couldn't have done anything. Could Hunter have anything to do with it? Now *that* would be a real twist. Especially since he was the one who wanted to hire her.

"Dacey was out to dinner with Greyson. And Hunter—"

"Whoa, Maison. Relax. I'm just trying to do my job here. And that includes questioning everyone. It doesn't mean I think they did it. I just have to make sure that they *didn't*."

Maison let out a relieved breath. "Okay, I just don't want people going around and talking shit about them behind their backs."

"I highly doubt that's going to happen."

"Hunter is already under a lot of pressure as it is now that he's taken his father's place."

"Huh, what?" *Did she just say—*

"You didn't hear?" Maison seemed supremely proud to know something that she didn't. "That's why there are so many people outside."

Sam stiffened. "What do you mean?" She glanced around. "What's going on?"

"Hunter is the new CEO of Gleam Enterprises."

FOUR

"WHEN THE HELL DID THIS HAPPEN?" *AND WHY hadn't he told her!*

"Just last night," Maison informed her. "He called me and told me he was stepping in. Today is actually his first day on the job. That's why all the people are outside."

What? She thought it was because news broke of the attempted murder! But this made more sense. What Sam didn't understand was why Hunter was doing this when she knew from his brother that he never had any interest in following in his father's footsteps?

Maison was smiling at her. "You seem a little shocked. Are you all right?"

"Is he—" Sam pointed to the door behind Maison. "Is he inside right now?" Should she go and talk to him?

Maison nodded. "I kept the doors closed because there's no doubt everyone will be wanting to speak with him about his father. I know he's had a rough time these last few days so I'm trying to make his first day as stress-free as possible."

Sam smiled at the other girl. "You're a really good friend."

Maison shrugged. "I'm just doing my job." Now if only the rest of Gleam's employees were as devoted as Maison was. Sam had a feeling that would make her job a lot easier. But with the enemies that Matthew had made over the years, she had a lot of ground to cover if she wanted to find out exactly what had happened that night. "Do you want to go inside and see him?" Maison asked.

Sam rose from her chair. "No, that's okay." She had nothing to report to him yet. And she doubted he'd want to see her while he was busy with work. She would just be a reminder of all the bad things that were happening in his life at the moment. "Thanks for all your help, Maison. I appreciate it."

"Sure, anytime. If you have any more questions, just give me a call."

"Thanks, will do."

But even as she left the building, Sam felt this unnerving feeling that she was still missing something.

Hunter's eyes were glued on his computer screen but nothing in his mind was clicking. How the hell did his father do this? All he saw were numbers and words that made no sense to him. It was only his first day at Gleam and already he could feel the walls closing in.

He was going to call Maison in and ask for some assistance but he could already hear that she was speaking to someone. Her soft voice rose and fell like a melody, and for a moment, he wondered who the hell was out there with her. Probably Hutch. Ever since the accident happened, Maison had said that his brother had grown more protective of her.

Instead of getting up to check, Hunter closed the window on his screen and stood up. Maybe walking around the office would clear his head a bit.

Already taking a break? His father would laugh at him.

From the fifty-fourth floor, Hunter glanced down at the reporters below. If he thought the people at the hospital were bad, this was ten times worse. These men and women all had questions for him. About his father. About his new decision to take over. About what was going to happen to Gleam Enterprises.

He was glad for Maison's presence because she could be

there to act as a buffer and guide him through. Hell, he'd be the first one to admit that he had no idea what he was doing.

Hunter tore his gaze away from the window and let out a long breath. His life was going to be a hell of a lot more different now that he carried this position of power. The coming days were no doubt going to be difficult but hopefully he'd learn to adjust and things would get easier. But he knew this decision would not only affect him but Owen as well. He had to make sure he kept his priorities straight. Despite the hundreds of people beneath him at the moment, no one was going to come before Owen.

The kid was his life. His everything. And since having a child, he now understood his father's protectiveness. Despite the fact that all of Matthew's children were adults now, a father never stopped caring about his family. Like him, he wanted to make sure his children had everything they needed and deserved.

His mind flitted back to his early morning. As always, Owen was having a hard time getting up but since it was his first day at Gleam, Hunter wanted to be early. He hadn't gotten a morning routine set in stone yet so the lunch packing and the getting ready part had all been hurried. But he still managed to get Owen dressed, fed, and out the door on time. Except . . .

"*Son of a bitch!*" Had he put Owen's lunch in his bag? Now that he thought about it, he was pretty sure his sandwich was still sitting on the kitchen countertop at home. "Shit," Hunter muttered as he glanced at the clock. He still had some time before noon. Maybe he could pick it up and bring it to him before then.

Maison looked surprised to see him as he came out of his office. "Hunter, is everything okay?"

"Everything is fine." He just felt like a terrible father. How could he forget his kid's lunch! "I'm just going to head over to Owen's school for a bit. Is that okay?"

"That's fine." He was glad she didn't ask him to stay because that wouldn't have gone well with him. While he may have volunteered to take this position on, this job was second to his duties to his son. To his surprise, Maison said, "You just missed Sam," as he walked past her.

Hunter froze and turned to her. "Sam? *Sam was here?*" *Why hadn't she come talk to him?*

"Yes. She came to ask me some questions."

"What did she say?"

"She seems to think that Clive might have something to do with what happened to your father. I told her she was crazy." All Hunter could do was purse his lips while Maison's gaze scanned his face. "Oh, come on!" she exclaimed. "You think he had something to do with it too? But he's been a friend of yours for years!"

"To be honest, I hardly know the man." Sure, they'd spoken on a few occasions before, but he could hardly say he was best friends with the guy. With a relationship as strained as his was with his father, spending time with his old man's business partner wasn't normally how he spent his afternoons. Maison shot him a look that told him she wasn't pleased with him. Actually, she looked utterly betrayed. "I just have her looking into some things okay," he explained. "And I'm worried about Dad. If she can help, then what's the harm? I'd appreciate it if you answer any questions she has. If Sam can get to the bottom of what happened that night, the quicker we can put this all to rest."

"Okay, fine," Maison said through clenched teeth.

"Thank you." Hunter headed for the ground floor in a hurry. As soon as he was through the main doors, cameras flashed and dozens of people shouted his name. Shit, for a moment there, he'd totally forgotten about them being out here.

Covering his face from the bright lights, Hunter kept his head down as he made his way to his car. Fucking hell, they were everywhere! It was a wonder how anyone else got in and out of the building. For a beat, he wondered how Sam fared. Was she as overwhelmed with this as he was?

God, he was in over his head, he thought as he headed home for Owen's lunch. His first day at his new job had unnerved him so much that he'd let his mind wander, causing him to forget his kid's lunch. Tomorrow, he was going to make sure he was better prepared. He didn't want Owen suffering like he was.

But he knew having a family required some sacrifices sometimes. Hunter just hoped that it wouldn't backfire on him. He had enough to deal with without shit blowing back in his face.

After lunch, Sam slid back into her black Honda Civic. Hutch had always made fun of her car, calling it "basic." But that was the point! As a private investigator, she *had* to blend in. She couldn't drive around Moonrise Beach in the flashy cars he liked. Also, a car this size was easy for her to make sharp turns in case things got hairy quick. It also got her from point A to point B. What more could she ask for?

After seeing Maison, Sam decided that she needed to see Clive too. Since she knew already that he wasn't at the office today, her best guess was that he was at home. Maybe she could have a little chat with him before the police came to question him. She was just about to pull onto the road when her phone rang. Hutch's name flashed on the screen. "Hey, how's your dad doing?" she said by way of greeting.

"Good. He woke up."

Sam perked up. "Really? Oh, thank God." She'd been so worried.

"Yeah, but the doctors still want to keep an eye on him so he'll stay in the hospital for a few more days."

"Did he mention anything about the accident?" She wanted to know if she could ask him some questions.

"No. He's still not talking much but I was so excited that I just went to see Maison."

Sam debated whether or not telling him that she'd just visited her too but decided it wasn't worth mentioning. Instead she asked, "So Hunter—"

Her friend's huffing laughter cut her off. "You heard too, huh?"

"Did he tell you that he was going to do that? I thought you said he refused your father."

"He did, but I guess he changed his mind."

"Why do you think he did it?"

"Your guess is as good as mine."

Hmm. Maybe things had changed for him. Maybe Hunter felt a certain obligation to his father. Or maybe he was doing it to prevent Clive from taking over.

She'd seen the look on his face when Deacon had told him about the brakes. Hunter hadn't admitted it but he'd looked afraid. Sam hated seeing him this way.

"Do you think he's doing it because he doesn't want Clive to take over?" She'd love to get another person's opinion. Maybe it would help her understand the case more.

"If what they're saying is true and someone did try to kill my dad . . ." Her best friend's voice trailed off and Sam realized her error too late. She was treating this with the same ease she did with every case. But this wasn't just a normal case for Hutch and Hunter. This was something personal.

Damn, what was wrong with her? She was so used to talking to Hutch about her cases that she forgot that this was his family they were talking about. How could she be so callous?

"I'm sorry," she said, even though she knew it was useless. Unless she could find out what exactly happened that night, her words held no meaning. Her hands tightened on the steering wheel. "I'm going to find out who did this," she told him. "I just need a little bit of time."

She thought she heard Hutch breathe out harshly on the other end of the line, and for a moment, she wondered if he was crying. But when Hutch spoke again, his voice was clear of emotion. "When are we going to hang out again? Want to make another trip to the gun range?"

A smile burst across her face. "I didn't think you'd want to go back."

"Why not?"

"I don't know. I just figured that since you're with Maison now—"

"Maison isn't like that. And besides, I miss you."

"Ugh. Don't get sappy with me."

"Would you rather that I call you names?"

"All right, all right," she snapped. "We'll hang out. I just have to go somewhere first."

"Where are you going?"

"To the place where it all started."

FIVE

TWENTY MINUTES LATER, HUNTER ARRIVED AT OWEN'S school. It was a good thing he'd arrived when he did because although he had some time before lunch started, he'd also come in time to see Owen throwing a massive hissy fit in his classroom. "What the—" He'd never seen him like this!

Ms. Poon, a lovely kindergarten teacher with a quiet disposition, was directing Owen to a chair but his son wasn't having any of it. Instead, Owen was kicking and screaming and crying like some beast was trapped inside of his small body. He fell to the ground and started thrashing, crying uncontrollably.

Shit.

Hunter didn't even bother knocking before he rushed into the room and knelt down by his son. "Hey. What's wrong?" Owen never behaved like this. Sure he had his tantrums sometimes but this seemed different.

For a moment, surprise filtered over his son's features before Owen fell into his arms and sobbed. Hunter ignored the looks from the other kids around him and shot an apologetic look at Owen's teacher. Ms. Poon seemed surprised at first to see him, but then relief spread over her features as he comforted Owen.

"I'm sorry to intrude, but I came to bring Owen his lunch," Hunter explained. He still held the brown bag in his hand. "I didn't mean to storm in."

"I'm glad you're here," Ms. Poon said. "Owen has been

acting a little strange today."

Strange? "What do you mean?"

"His focus has been off and I've noticed that he hasn't been playing with the other children as much."

What? Owen was normally a well-tempered kid but he'd have his meltdowns every now and then. Recently though, Hunter had noticed that Owen was getting more clingy and complained of headaches and stomachaches more often. He also had a hard time getting him to sleep at night and waking up in the morning. But was this all a result of what was happening in their lives? Would taking this job at Gleam worsen things with Owen? Fear put him in a stranglehold and worry for his son made him feel like crying.

Hunter forced himself to look at his teacher. "Could I stay with him for a moment until he calms down? I promise I won't linger around afterwards."

Ms. Poon smiled down at him. "Of course. I'm surprised you're even here after the news broke this morning."

"Ah, yeah." He rubbed the back of his neck awkwardly, suddenly embarrassed. Would people treat him differently now that he was a CEO? "Well, my kid comes first."

"Can't argue with that. Would you like a chair to sit in?"

"That would be great. Thanks." Hunter pulled Owen closer to him, ignoring his sobs as he settled himself into the nearest chair. Owen was squeezing his neck like a python. "Whoa, Owen. Relax. We're just going to sit down at the table. I've brought you lunch. Do you want to see?"

"No! I want to go home." The death grip around his neck tightened until it became a chore to breathe.

"Sorry," Hunter wheezed. "But you've still got a lot of fun stuff to do here. We can't go home yet."

"I wanna go hooome!" Owen howled.

"Don't you want some lunch?" Hunter reached for the bag and pulled out the sandwich. Owen *loved* sandwiches. If given the opportunity, he would eat them for breakfast, lunch, and dinner.

"No, I don't want to eat! I want to go HOME!" His next yell was so loud, Ms. Poon jumped beside him. Hunter rubbed his ear. *Ow. That hurt.*

Okay. Something was up. Owen rarely threw hissy fits like this. Worst of all, he had no idea what to do to stop it.

All the other kids were looking at them, making the heat rise up his neck. "Look, Owen, I'm not sure what happened but this isn't how we act when we're at school. Here." He pushed the sandwich in front of him. "Eat this, okay? I brought it especially for you." He smiled but Owen wasn't even looking at his face. His head was tilted down, eyes trained on his shoes as tears ran down his chubby cheeks.

Damn, it fucking broke his heart to see him this way but every kid had to go to school, right? Owen was here to learn and play with other kids. *I'm sorry, little guy.* But he had to stay in school.

The moment he rose to his full height, Owen shot up and wrapped his arms around his legs. "Whoa, what are you—" He pitched forward but caught himself before he landed on his kid's teacher.

"Take me home, take me home," Owen begged. *"I wanna go hoooooooome."*

Hunter gently took hold of him and placed him back in the chair. His voice was stern when he said, "Owen, we'll go home later but for now you have to stay here."

"Nooooo!" More crying drowned out his words.

Hunter was out of options. When he turned to Ms. Poon, she shot him a sympathetic look. "Why don't you let me talk to him?" she suggested.

What? What could she say to him that he hadn't already? And why would he listen to his teacher over his own father? The part of him that wanted to protect his son wanted to refuse her but Hunter bit back his frustration and allowed her to take the lead. Maybe she could offer him something that he couldn't. With a nod, he stepped away, hiding the fact that his hands shook.

Ms. Poon kept a respectable distance from Owen as she sat down beside him, but even then, her words had the same effect of a warm, comforting embrace. Soon, Owen's ragged breaths lessened and his crying eventually stopped. Why hadn't he stopped crying for him?

As Hunter stood in the doorway to the classroom, he did his best to control his roiling emotions. This day had made him into a ball of emotion. He thought that in seeing his son, he'd feel better. But now, he felt even worse than before. Would his days get progressively worse from here?

His gaze returned to Ms. Poon and his son. Owen had lifted his tiny head and wiped his wet face with the back of his sleeve. His entire face was red from crying, and his small lips trembled as he spoke. "I want my mommy," he whispered, and beside him, Hunter saw Ms. Poon stiffen.

He, on the other hand, stopped breathing altogether. *Fucking hell.* He knew the day would come when Owen would ask for his mother; he just didn't realize how hard it was going to be when it did.

Whatever Ms. Poon had said to him next worked in comforting him further because Owen wiped his nose, turned to his lunch, and started to eat. The teacher rose to her full height and glanced back at him. She didn't say anything though and Hunter was glad that she hadn't. He felt like he had failed his son.

Bringing his hands together, he thanked her silently for what she'd done for his child. And although it killed him to do it, Hunter forced himself to turn away. He didn't want to admit it, but Owen had just shattered his heart when he'd said those four small words. What if he couldn't provide him with everything that he needed in life? What if there would always be something missing?

With a heavy heart, Hunter walked back to his car and started his long drive back to Gleam.

Clive Davenport's home wasn't too far away from where the Happa-Hewitts lived so Sam didn't have too much trouble locating it. Her biggest obstacle would be getting Clive to talk to her when he likely didn't want to talk to anyone at this point. But Sam wouldn't be good at her job if she at least didn't try to see him. She had to know if he wanted to take control of the company badly enough to want to eliminate Matthew.

It took a while for someone to answer the door for her but she was thrilled to see the real Clive Davenport before her. Up until now, she'd only seen images and videos of the man who co-owned Gleam Enterprises. "Can I help you?" he asked her.

Sam immediately slid into character. "Hello, Mr. Davenport, I'd like to ask you some questions about Matthew Hewitt's accident."

Clive looked dumbfounded. "Who are you?"

"My name is Sam Cosi."

"And you're investigating Matthew's accident?" He sounded wary. "Are you with the Moonrise Beach Police Department?" He looked her up and down. "I hope you don't take this the wrong way, but you don't look like a cop."

Sam grinned, not at all offended. She liked her style and

black was always in fashion. "I'm a private investigator." She held out her hand and Clive shook it.

"Can I ask who hired you?"

"I'm not at liberty to say. But I'd really like to ask you some questions. Are you available now?"

Clive worried his bottom lip. "I suppose so." Stepping back, he allowed her entry. Sam didn't hesitate as she stepped into the shiny foyer.

"Thank you." She expected him to put up more of a fight but Clive Davenport actually had a pleasant disposition. She could believe what Maison had said about him being well liked in the company. But he could always change his mind and ask her to leave at any time so she had to tread lightly.

Her sharp eyes took in everything at once. She'd never been in a house this nice before, and although she was pretty sure Hutch now lived in something like this, she'd never once set foot in his father's home. He'd always just come to her place if he wanted to hang out with her.

The shiny marbled floors made her boots look extra ugly and scuffed up and Sam debated whether or not she should take them off. In the end, she opted for keeping them on in case she needed to make a quick getaway.

"Let's talk here," Clive said as he led her to a room filled with books. Sam supposed this was his library and the area where he spent most of his time when he wasn't at the office. Books lined the entire perimeter, giving it a homey look she enjoyed. If given the chance, Sam would've spent an entire evening discovering what worlds lay hidden away on these shelves. As her gaze continued to scan the surroundings, her eyes landed on a couple of comfy-looking chairs. "Can we?" she asked, indicating the seat before her.

Clive nodded. "Please."

As she sat down, she studied Clive more closely. The older man looked like what she supposed a normal 56-year-old would look like. He had gray hair and crinkled skin but instead of looking old and haggard, the wrinkles gave him a classy, distinguished look. Clive also had a hooked nose and large hands, hands that were now folded together in his lap. She didn't know if that was a product of her presence here or if he usually sat like that, all tense and poised all at the same time. "I'd like to ask you a few questions now, if that's okay."

Clive didn't express his assent but he didn't refuse either so Sam jumped straight into the first question. "I want to know more about the night of the accident. Did you feel or see anything strange? Was Matthew acting differently than his usual self?"

"No, not at all. We chatted like we always do. We're old friends, you see, so when we're together we're speaking a mile a minute."

Sam smiled. "What did you two talk about?"

"Mostly about work. About some of the people we've had to work with."

Had something happen at work that may have triggered this whole thing? "Anyone in particular?"

"Matthew was complaining about this one guy."

"Who was the person?" If Matthew was upset with him or her, then perhaps this person may have played a part in his accident later on that night.

"His name is Brian Melwood. He's fairly new to the company and he and Matthew tend to butt heads quite a bit."

"What happened?"

"It's just business really. Brian is in charge of Gleam's international affairs and wanted to expand business in other countries, but Matthew wasn't going for it."

"Do you think that would cause Brian to want to hurt Matthew in any way?" Although she'd come to investigate Clive, she wasn't stupid enough to ignore other possibilities.

Clive waved off the suggestion. "No. No way. Our business is cutthroat, but I don't think it'd give anyone a reason to want another person dead."

"Not even you?"

"Me?" Clive's eyes bulged out.

"Yes. You didn't try to kill Matthew, did you?"

"Absolutely not! He's my best friend, my business partner. Why would I ever want any harm to come to him?"

She was playing bad cop now. Maybe it would shake something loose. "If something were to happen to him, you'd be in charge of everything."

"I'm not," he argued. "As you can plainly see, I'm not even at the office. His son Hunter is taking his father's place for the time being."

So he knew about Hunter. Sam wondered how he felt about that. "Do you want to be the one running things in his absence?"

"Of course I do. Hunter has no clue what he's doing. But because he's next in line, he can step in and I can't do anything about it!"

"You sound upset."

"Of course I'm upset!" Clive snapped. No longer stoic, the older man radiated anger. "Instead of trying to smooth things out at the office, I'm stuck here, waiting for the cops to arrive because they think I tried to kill someone."

His emotions looked genuine, but Sam had been fooled before. Unfortunately, she had no evidence to pin on Clive other than a few words heard by someone else. "Okay, Mr. Davenport. I appreciate you talking to me." She rose and started for the door but she froze when she heard a sound. "What was that?"

Clive was already behind her. When she heard the sound again, she quickly came face-to-face with another man.

The man's sandy-brown hair looked a lot like straw beneath his faded baseball hat and his ruddy complexion was made even more flushed-looking by the presence of pimples scattered around his face. While he was a little on the heavy side, she pegged him to be in his late twenties, maybe even early thirties.

"Mickey," Clive growled from behind her. "Where the hell have you been?"

"I was out. Got a problem with that?"

Mickey? Shit. She should've done more research. She had no idea Clive's son, Michael, was back in town. "What are you looking at?" he snapped as she pinned him with a gaze. Sam arched a brow.

Ah. What lovely manners he had.

Suddenly, the doorbell rang. "Answer the door, Mickey," Clive ordered.

"You answer it," he snapped back. "I just got here." When Mickey walked down the hall, away from the front door, Clive cursed.

"Excuse me," he muttered. "I need to answer that."

"Sure, you go ahead." Sam had her eyes on his son now. Maybe he could tell her more about his father. While Clive was distracted, she quickly followed Mickey down the hall. "Sorry to interrupt your"—Sam glanced at the clock and realized that a good chunk of the afternoon had passed—"lunch, but I was wondering if I could ask you a few questions."

Mickey peered out from behind the fridge door. "Don't you know it's rude to wander around someone else's house?"

"Ah, sorry." She really wasn't but she figured it was best to stay on Mickey's good side if she wanted any answers from him.

"What do you want?" he snapped as he picked up a knife and violently stabbed it into the mayo bottle like it was a piece of carcass. He then spread some on a slice of bread before him.

"I just wanted to ask about your father and his involvement with the accident."

"Why? What happened?" His expression morphed from confusion to anger in a second. "And who are you?"

"I'm Sam Cosi. I'm a private investigator. Your father is the lead suspect of an attempted murder case that I'm investigating."

Mickey's eyes bulged out of his head. "What the fuck? Are you serious?"

"You aren't aware of the accident?"

"No. What the hell? My dad?"

Sam nodded. "He's been friends with Matthew for a very long time. What do you know of him?"

"Matthew? Uhh. I don't know. He'd old like my dad," he said, as if that meant something.

Damn, this wasn't going to be easy. This Mickey guy seemed clueless about everything. How had he not heard about the accident? It was all over the news!

Behind her, Sam could hear the sound of familiar voices and she realized with a start that Deacon must've come to take Clive in for an interview. It was a good thing she got here before they did.

She turned back to Mickey. "We all thought it was an accident at first," she told him. "It was raining hard and we know that he swerved to avoid hitting something, but the police believe that something happened to the brakes as well."

Mickey shook his head. "Sorry, lady, but I don't have a clue.

I hardly talk to the guy." Sam bit back a retort. She hated when men called her *lady*. No matter how you said it, it just sounded so condescending. "What if he just had crap reflexes?" Mickey remarked. "My dad is like that too. Can't stop quick enough to save his life."

Matthew isn't dead, Sam wanted to correct but she stopped herself. It would only start an argument. "Anyway, thanks for talking to me. I'll let myself out."

Mickey didn't spare her with another response; he simply bit into his sandwich.

Returning to the hallway, Sam pasted on a smile as she came face-to-face with Deacon and another cop she knew well, Juliana Michaels. "Ah, there you are," Clive said. "The Moonrise Beach Police are here."

Although Deacon nodded at her, he didn't say anything as their eyes met. "I can see that. Great to see you again."

Clive looked between them. "You guys know each other?"

Sam smiled. "Something like that. Anyway, I'd better go. Thanks for your time, Mr. Davenport."

Clive opened his mouth to say something but Sam was already out the door. She didn't want to admit it, but she kind of felt bad for the guy. While she wasn't quite sure he was the one who had tried to kill Matthew, she'd be a fool to dismiss him so early in the game.

SIX

HUNTER HAD RETURNED TO GLEAM, BUT ALTHOUGH his body was here physically, his mind wasn't. He was still thinking about Owen and his agonized words. Quite honestly, he wished he'd never heard it. It stung more than it should have.

He thought that he'd always been a good parent for his kid. While he'd made his fair share of mistakes, he never thought that his son lacked in anything. But of course, every kid needed a mother and that was a void that he would never be able to fill on his own.

As if that wasn't enough to deal with, he still had to learn to adjust to his new job. Thankfully, when he'd returned Maison had told him that his father was awake now so that gave him confidence that things would be okay. Now all he had to do was make it through his workdays here. But that was easier said than done.

Hunter focused back on his monitor and the piles of paper before him. He'd always made fun of his father's work, saying that all he did was play solitaire behind his desk all day when actually his workload probably weighed double—maybe even triple—his weight in total. He understood now why he and Maison always worked so late into the evenings.

Speaking of Maison, he'd wanted to ask her something about a file he had. He just—"Dammit." Where had he put it? He scanned his desk for the piece of paper, but his entire desk was swimming in files already. "Shit. Don't tell me I lost it."

That would be just the thing to make his day even worse.

Hunter stood up, figuring that it might help him locate the file easier when his gaze landed on another piece of paper. "What the hell?" It was an invoice for his father's mechanic. He checked the date and realized that it was from a week before the accident had occurred. He scanned down to see what it was that the mechanic had worked on. Looked like his father had done a routine check and the mechanic had billed him two hundred bucks for it.

While he had no idea if this was relevant to the case, he figured he'd better bring it to Sam's attention in case it might help her figure out what was going on. Pulling out his phone, he called her, his work once again forgotten.

As his phone rang, a flurry of butterflies took flight in his gut, which surprised him since he had no reason to be nervous with Sam. But as the phone rang and he clutched the piece of paper in his hand, he couldn't deny that he was desperate to hear the sound of her voice.

Sam had just pulled up at Gleam when her phone rang. "Hunter? Is that you?" He'd never called her before but since programming his number into her phone, his name now flashed on the screen.

"Hey, yeah, it's me."

"What's wrong? Is everything okay?"

"Everything is fine," he assured her in a voice that was smooth as silk. *Damn, what was it about this man's voice that got to her?* "So I found something that I think might help your investigation." The warm fuzzy feelings she had at hearing his voice were gone in a flash.

"What is it?"

"It might be nothing, but I found an invoice to a garage

that my father likes to use. He had the car checked out by a guy named Diego at a place called Fix Auto."

"When is the invoice dated?"

"About a week ago. Think it's worth checking out? It might be nothing, but I—"

"No, no. I'll check it out. I've just pulled up to Gleam. I'll come by your office after I finish up what I plan to do and pick it up. I'd like to see the invoice in person myself."

"Wait. You're here?"

"I was actually here this morning too but figured you'd be too busy to see me."

"Not at all. Come by whenever you want." Her heart skipped a beat at the open invitation. "But may I ask, what other business do you have here?"

"I'm following up on a lead."

"A lead? Do tell."

"Well, I just spoke with Clive and he told me that your father had an argument with Brian Melwood. Sound familiar?"

"Brian? Wow, you really are good."

"Huh?" Sam was thrown off by the sudden change in topic. "What are you talking about?"

"Sorry, I didn't mean to make you uncomfortable. I'm just glad you're helping me." The words warmed her and Sam found herself smiling stupidly in her car. She forced herself to stop and focus back on the case.

"So what do you think? Could Brian Melwood have done something to your father?"

"I don't know. My father regularly got into arguments with a lot of people. If you don't know, he's not exactly a well liked man."

Yeah, she was quickly gathering that. But she didn't want to intentionally leave a stone unturned only to realize that she'd made the mistake by looking the other way. "I'm still going to take a quick look. I won't be long," she added, knowing that it was getting late and he'd probably want to head home in the next hour or so.

"Don't worry about me. I'll be here."

"Okay." But she still didn't want to keep him waiting. After hanging up, Sam quickly walked up to the building and asked to see Mr. Melwood. She was asked to wait, but at least the crowd out front had lessened a little bit. She was able to squeeze by again without being apprehended.

When her name was called, Sam jumped to her feet, following the secretary down a long hallway until they stopped at a big office. Brian Melwood glanced up from his desk and smiled at her. Sam didn't waste any time. "Hi, Mr. Melwood. I'm sorry to come here unannounced, but I would like to ask you some questions about Matthew Hewitt."

"Certainly. Have a seat." The secretary left and, suddenly, Sam was left alone with the man. Brian Melwood usually handled the international side of things at Gleam, so she knew he was a busy man. And since Hunter was waiting for her too, Sam cut straight to the chase. "I was told that you and Mr. Hewitt got into an argument recently," she began.

Brian's smile was kind. "Ah yes, we butt heads from time to time. But that's pretty normal between us."

"What are your thoughts about Matthew? I heard you're still pretty new to the company."

"I've been here for only a year and, yes, he's my biggest competitor when it comes to ideas. We don't always see eye to eye on things." Sam examined him. He didn't look very much like a notable character. He had a medium build and dark hair and eyes but there was nothing about him that struck her as odd or out of the ordinary. She also liked how open he was with her. But openness didn't equate to innocence.

"Can you tell me where you were the night of the accident?"

A smile curled Brian's lips. "Are you a cop? You told my secretary that you were a private investigator, but you seem more like a cop."

"No, I'm not a cop. But I'm sure they'll come around to ask you questions as well. Please answer the question, sir."

Brian sighed. "I was having dinner with my wife. If you or the police require proof, you can talk to my wife and the restaurant. They know me well and I'm sure they can verify the time that I was there."

"Thanks. I'll do that." So far, this visit was going smoothly, a much better improvement than when she'd tried to interview Mickey. "Can I ask what you two fought about the day of the accident?"

"Oh, the usual. I've been trying to convince him to expand but Matthew likes keeping things close to where he can keep an eye on things. He's hard to trust and sometimes, it affects the company."

"So your argument with him wasn't out of the ordinary for you two?"

"Not at all. We've been at each other's throat since I started working for him." Brian smiled. "It would be more strange if we actually agreed on something."

Sam rose and nodded her thanks. "That's all I wanted to ask. Thanks for your time." Although it'd been quick, Sam felt like she'd wasted a great deal of his time. If Brian's alibi checked out, then she'd have no reason to suspect. Still, she had to be careful.

Brian pulled out a business card and handed it to her. "If you have any more questions, you can contact me here."

"Thanks." Sam took the card and put it in her pocket.

Damn. That felt more anticlimactic than she anticipated. What if Clive had tried to trick her by pointing someone else out? She had to know how his interview went with the police. Dashing back to her car, she immediately called Deacon. Sam wasn't surprised to hear his voice after the first ring. "What happened with Clive's interview?" she said by way of greeting.

Amusement tinged Deacon's voice. "I was wondering when I was going to hear from you."

"Stop flirting and tell me what happened," she snapped.

Deacon chuckled but cut right to the chase. "Well, he denies his involvement in the accident. He talked about this guy—"

"Brian Melwood."

"Yeah. We're going to check on him next—"

"Don't bother. I just went to see him."

"Damn, Sam. Can't you leave me something?" Deacon whined.

"Well, you are the lead investigator on this case. You check him out and tell me what you think."

"I will." Deacon huffed. "But something tells me that I would be wasting my time."

"I felt like I had," she admitted.

"Dammit, so what do you think? Hunter told me that he hired you. Why?"

"He tried to. I turned him down."

"So why the hell were you at Clive's today?"

"I'm doing it as a favor for Hutch."

"Ah, I see." There was a rustle as Deacon let out a long breath. "I feel really bad about what happened."

"Me too. But I'll help in any capacity I can. I'd like it if you shared your information with me. And I'll do the same for you."

"You got it." This wouldn't be the first time they helped each other. As a police detective, Deacon had resources that she didn't have. But Sam had good instincts and investigative skills that Deacon found useful from time to time. It was why they remained good friends.

"So, it's getting late. What are your plans for tonight?"

Sam already had a smile in place. "I'm meeting with Hunter to talk about the case."

"*Hunter?* Wow, so you found out that he's going to be the next CEO of Gleam Enterprises and now you're going to see him? You're moving quick." Her smile widened. Was that jealously she was hearing in his voice?

"It's not like that. We're going to talk about the case."

"If that was the case, he should be calling *me*."

Sam laughed. "You sound so jealous."

"Maybe I am. Why don't you go out with me?"

"Calm down, I'm not going out with him. He's a client."

"You just said that he wasn't."

"You know what I mean!"

"So you like him?"

Sam blew out an annoyed breath. "God, you're so annoying. I'm hanging up now."

Deacon's laugh carried through the line. "So you do! I know you, Sam Cosi. If you weren't interested in him, you would've told him to take a hike."

"I told you, I'm doing it for Hutch."

"Why aren't you going to see Hutch then?"

"I don't need to listen to this," she snapped. "I already have my mother breathing down my back because of this wedding."

"I told you already, I'll go with you if you can't find someone else."

"But you're a cop!"

"What's wrong with me being a cop?"

"Nothing, but if my mom found out, it would give her a stroke."

"Not sexy enough for her? Ouch. Okay then, what about Hunter? He must wear a suit now. I thought she liked men in suits."

"I'm not going to ask Hunter!"

"What about Hutch?"

"Hutch has a girlfriend already." And although Maison was sweet, she didn't think she'd let her boyfriend go to a wedding as someone else's date.

"Guess you're stuck with me then." Sam closed her eyes in exasperation. She could just picture Deacon's feline smile on the other end of the line.

"Unfortunately, I am. Let's just hope my mother doesn't think you're a complete wiener when she sees your—"

"Hey!"

Sam cackled as Deacon shot into a million arguments.

"I'm kidding. Relax. I'm sure it's fine. Not that I have any intention of finding out so don't even try."

"Aw, you're no fun."

"Anyway, I gotta go."

"Mr. Grey awaits!"

"I can't believe you just said that." CEO or not, she doubted Hunter was like that. So why then did she suddenly feel like her libido was about to start talking to her? "God," she muttered as she hung up on Deacon. She *so* needed to get laid.

SEVEN

"**H**EY, MAISON. I'M SORRY FOR COMING AROUND unannounced again." Although it was much later in the day, Maison still had a smile in place for her.

"It's fine. I planned on staying late anyway."

Sam glanced at the door behind her and a shiver of excitement ran through her. "Is he in there?"

Maison nodded and tipped her head toward the door. "Go right inside."

"Thanks." Knocking twice before peeking her head into the office, she said, "Hi, it's me."

Behind the huge desk in the center of a glass room, Hunter grinned at her. The dazzling smile blindsided her and Sam felt the impact as if he'd thrown a football into her chest. It must've been the sunlight pouring in through the floor-to-ceiling windows because Hunter looked as bright and as shiny as a diamond as he came around the desk to greet her. "Wow," she breathed. "You look—"

A dimple appeared in his cheeks before he looked down at himself. "I know, right?" He looked *very* different from the last time she'd seen him. He'd ditched the T-shirt and jeans ensemble for a beautifully tailored gray suit. Gone were the dirty old boots too; he now wore perfectly polished shoes that gleamed like gossamer wings. She would've thought that with his bulk and size, a suit would look ridiculous on him but it was clear Hunter Happa-Hewitt was capable of pulling off any look. Now

Sam understood her mother's obsession with men in suits. She could get used to seeing Hunter all dressed up like this.

Hunter fingered the collar at his throat before reaching out for her. "Come have a seat." To her surprise, he took her hand and guided her to one of the chairs before his desk. "I'm really glad you came," he said as he settled back down in his seat.

Sam found herself grinning. And to be honest, she was a little flustered too. He was treating her like a superior guest. "So how's the new job?"

Hunter made a face. "Let's just say it's not what I expected."

Her smile grew. "Regretting it already?"

"No." He said it with no hesitation at all. "I just have to get used to it, that's all. So how was your visit with Brian?"

Now it was her turn to make a face. "I'm still deciding about him. He seems like a nice guy but I can't ignore the fact that he had an argument with your father right before the accident."

Hunter frowned. "Yeah, the fact that my father has a lot of enemies doesn't make this any easier." He reached for a paper on his desk. "Here's the invoice."

She took the piece of paper from him and examined it. "Does your dad visit this mechanic often?"

"Yes. He's meticulous about his cars."

Well, if that was the case, then she may have to pay a visit to this shop. "Do you mind if I keep this?"

"Not at all. It's yours. Do you plan on checking them out?"

"Yes. I can't be sure that it'll be helpful at this point. But since the brakes were tampered with, maybe this Diego Garcia guy knows something we don't."

"Thanks. That helps a lot. I appreciate you doing this for me."

"Like I said, I'm doing it as a favor for—"

"My brother. I know. But I'm still grateful." His voice held such sincerity that Sam caught his gaze.

Hunter held it for several seconds until Sam felt her cheeks begin to flush. She broke the trance and cleared her throat. "So how's Owen handling all this?"

A dark lens fell over Hunter's eyes. He blew out a frustrated breath as he leaned back in his chair. "Owen is having a tough time right now."

"What? What do you mean? Is he okay?"

Hunter seemed to find her concern for his son to be amusing because his lips quirked into a small smile. She hadn't been able to spend much time with Owen since they'd last seen each other but, strangely, Sam found herself missing the little guy.

"He threw a massive hissy fit this morning at school. Like it was Naomi Campbell–level hissy fit. Nothing I did could calm him down."

"Oh no. I'm so sorry to hear that." The words felt totally inadequate but what else could she offer him? She wasn't a mother. She had no insider's knowledge on how to care for a child. Hell, half the time she couldn't even manage to take care of herself let alone a small human being.

"Yeah." Hunter sounded dejected. "The worst part is, he asked for his mother."

Sam stiffened. *Oh shit.* She didn't have to be there to know how much that would've hurt. The sudden need to run around the table separating them consumed her and she wanted to pull Hunter into her arms and comfort him. After all that he'd been through, he didn't need to deal with this on top of it. "Have you thought about contacting his mother?" she asked.

Hunter shook his head. "No. I don't want anything to do with her." His pain was evident in the way his brows knitted together and his fists clenched tightly on top of the desk.

"I'm sorry. If there's something you think I can help with,

just let me know."

His eyes landed on her again and instead of seeing pain and frustration, she saw surprise. "Really?"

"Yes, of course." She liked Owen and enjoyed spending time with him.

"If you really mean that, I would really appreciate some help. I used to think I've done a pretty good job at raising Owen on my own but now I'm thinking if there are things I've missed. Things I can never give him."

Sam hated the sound of heartbreak in his voice. It was clear that he was doing his best and still feeling the heavy weight of life's stresses on him. Taking on this new job would only add to that. "You know what I think you need?" she said.

"What?"

"I think you need a day off."

Hunter's lips curled into a smirk. "It's only my first day, you know."

"I know, but you're clearly pushing yourself too hard.

"I think you should do something for yourself. Even if it's just for an evening."

"An evening to wind down," he mused aloud. "Man, it's been a long time since I've indulged like that."

"See? It'll be a nice change of pace for you. A chance to recharge."

Hunter turned to her suddenly. "What do you do to relax?"

A smile curled her lips. "You don't want to know."

"Really? Is it like a bubble bath or something like that?"

Her eyes flashed at his teasing tone. "No. No bubble baths. I like to shoot guns."

Hunter's bark of laughter echoed off the walls. He was grinning at her and she felt herself smile back. "I should've known. You probably frequent there often with the amount of hours you work then."

"I do. Especially since my baby sister is getting married soon and my mother has been trying to set me up with random men."

"Really? Mothers still do that?"

"Oh, you have no idea. She's been pushing a new guy on me every week!"

"That's quite an active dating life you've got there."

"Trust me," she said sternly. "I don't *want* to date them. Sometimes I go just to appease my mother. Other times I just blow them off."

Hunter winced. "So you're a heartbreaker . . ."

Pssht. "Trust me. Men don't see me as anything other than a friend most of the time."

"Don't be so sure." He'd said it on a whisper, but it had the same effect on her as if he'd yelled it to the ceiling. She was startled enough that she looked him in the eyes, surprised to find them glittering like onyx.

A flush rose high on her chest and she shot to her feet, breaking the moment. "Anyways, I better go."

Like a true gentleman, Hunter rose as well and walked her to the door. "Thanks for coming by," he said, voice smooth as silk. "I hope you find something useful there." He pointed at the invoice she clutched in her hands. "And if not, I'm sorry for wasting your time."

"You're not wasting my time." In fact, Sam was enjoying every minute spent with him. Probably more than she should.

With one last hurried smile, Sam wished him and his family well before saying goodnight and heading back to her car.

Hunter didn't do this. He didn't usually fall for a woman

so easily, but he'd been enraptured by Sam from the very first moment he'd seen her. Seeing her again now had reminded him of how different she was to the other women he was normally around. She'd walked in with her ripped jeans and leather jacket, looking more like Joan Jett than the Audrey Hepburns of his world and had snared his attention without any effort at all. He liked that about her. Liked how everything she did seemed so effortlessly cool and composed. It was a nice contrast to the chaos that was his life at the moment.

He watched her approach her car from the window, feeling something bloom inside of his chest. He wasn't an idiot. She'd been affected by his presence just as he had with her. What did that mean? Was she interested in him? And how could a woman like her believe that no man wanted her? He was surprised no one had tried to marry her already. But then again, Sam Cosi wouldn't get married to anyone unless she was ready.

Smiling, he thought about what it would be like to have an evening alone with Sam. That would be his ideal way to relax and enjoy himself, but he thought that if he brought it up with her, she'd go running and screaming in the other direction.

No, he had to pace himself. Despite the fury of feelings he had for Sam, he didn't have time for this.

Hell, he had so much on his plate right now that he couldn't even think straight. And if he threw Sam into the mix, well, that would just complicate things even more. He'd have to be patient and take his time. And then maybe after this was all over, he could finally ask Sam out.

He was pulled out of his thoughts when there was a soft knock on the door. Maison poked her head through and frowned when she didn't find him behind his desk. "Oh!

There you are. Are you ready to head home?"

Hunter glanced at the clock. He didn't realize how late it was. He still had to cook dinner for everyone. "Yeah, let's go home."

"Hutch invited me over for dinner. I hope that's okay."

Damn, that meant he'd have to make more. But that was okay; he loved having Maison around. "Of course it's okay."

"Dacey said she'd be there too. She's bringing Chinese takeout so you don't have to cook."

"Well, thank God," he breathed. He was exhausted.

Maison grinned at him. "Come on. Let's go home."

* * *

As he walked through the front door, the scent of Chinese take-out greeted him. His stomach growled in response but overriding that need was his desire to see Owen. Hunter's eyes scanned the living room for him but he wasn't there. He turned to the kitchen but didn't see him amongst his siblings and Maison. "Hey, where is—"

"He's upstairs," Hutch told him.

"Why?" Owen didn't like being upstairs alone.

Hutch shrugged. "He said he was tired."

Tired? Frowning, Hunter made a beeline for Owen's bedroom. He found his kid curled up under the covers, one arm wrapped around his favorite toy. His worry for him and momentary panic had made him forget all about his growling stomach as he quietly approached the bed and dropped down beside it.

Hunter checked to see if he was running a fever but the kid seemed perfectly fine.

Tired, Hutch had said. But Owen was a healthy five-year-old.

Why was he in bed before dinner?

His sister, Dacey, appeared in the doorway a moment later. "Is everything okay?" she asked.

"Huh? Oh yeah. He's sleeping right now. I think he's just tired."

Two lines of worry appeared between Dacey's brows but she didn't say anything other than, "Want me to save you two some dinner?"

"Yes, please. That would be great." Suddenly, Hunter had no appetite to eat. All he wanted to do right now was curl up in bed with his son and relax. These few precious moments would be just what he needed after a long day at work.

And within moments, he was fast asleep.

EIGHT

THE NEXT MORNING, SAM WOKE BRIGHT AND EARLY. She was just about to get into her car when Hutch called. "Hey, what are you doing today? Want to go to the gun range?" he asked.

"Sorry, I'd love to but I'm actually on my way to Auto Fix."

"So you're finally getting that piece of shit car fixed, huh?"

"*Bite your tongue*," she snarled. "I'm following up on a lead."

All teasing was dropped as Hutch sobered. "You mean for Dad's case?"

"Yeah, Hunter found an invoice on his desk yesterday. Thought it might give us some insight on what actually happened that night."

"You think it'll help?"

"That's what I'm trying to find out." She'd just managed to slip inside her car and turn on the engine. Stuffing the phone between her right cheek and shoulder, she clicked her seatbelt into place.

"Well, maybe you can also inquire about getting an upgrade on your car." Great. The teasing was back.

"My car is fine," she snapped as she put him on speakerphone and started to reverse.

"Might be nice to get the a/c fixed too."

"I can roll the windows down." Plus, she didn't have the budget right now to. "Is there a reason why you called, or did you just want to annoy me again?"

"I just want to know how my brother's doing."

"You live with him. Can't you check on him yourself?"

"He says he's fine, but I don't know if that's true or not." He began to tell her what happened when he'd come home last night and how Owen had been acting differently too.

"Yeah. He mentioned Owen to me."

"So you know that something is wrong. The frustrating thing is, I don't know how to help them." Although her gaze was focused on the road ahead of her, she smiled. "Hello?" Hutch said when she remained silent. "Are you still there?"

"Yeah, I'm here. I'm just a bit surprised, that's all." It amused her to see him worrying about his older brother like a mother hen.

"What the hell are you talking about?"

"I've never seen you worked up like this over your family." Well, technically she had every time he came to her to complain about his overbearing father, his annoying sister, and hardheaded brother. But this was different. This was Hutch worrying over his family because he cared about them.

"What about Dacey? How is she doing?"

"I think she's okay. She's been spending a hell of a lot more time at the house than she normally used to. It's kind of nice actually."

"That does sound good." Without him even realizing it, his family was growing closer and closer each day. She wondered if Hunter noticed it as well.

"I'll feel better once Dad is out of the hospital."

"Any word on when that will happen?" She wanted to see him and maybe ask some questions, but she figured she'd do what she could on her own before she bothered him while he was still recovering.

"The doctors say soon, but it feels like forever."

Hearing the worry in her best friend's voice, she said, "Don't worry. Everything will be fine."

"Are you driving right now?"

"Yes. You're on speakerphone."

"I'll leave you alone," Hutch said. "But we need to hang out soon. Feels like forever since we've last chilled together."

"We will," she promised. Maybe when she finished up here, she'd go and see him.

After saying her goodbyes, Sam focused back on the road. She'd gotten up particularly early this morning to avoid morning rush hour but things were still moving at a snail's pace.

Forty minutes later, she was walking up to the garage, her patience nearing the end of its leash. Traffic always set her off and she'd been a victim of road rage ever since she'd gotten her driver's permit at age sixteen.

She slowed when she realized that there was no one around. "Shit." Were they even open? She checked her watch. It was already nine. Why wasn't anyone here? "Hello?" she called out. "Is anyone here?"

When there was no response, Sam cursed again. It would be just her luck to come all this way and have the place be closed for the day.

With no one to question, she started to look around. Though she doubted it, maybe there was something left out that could help her answer some of her questions. But Auto Fix looked like every other garage she'd been in. Bottles of oil were lined up on the walls. Tires and tools dotted the perimeter. A clue could be sitting right in front of her and she would've overlooked it because she really had no clue about cars at all.

When two cars came rolling into the parking lot, Sam thought that the owner had finally arrived. But when the drivers approached, it was clear that they were looking to get their car serviced. She was just about to tell them that no one was here when a voice sounded behind her.

"Hello, can I help you?"

Sam spun around to find a Hispanic man emerging from the back room. "Sorry," he said as he wiped his hands clean on a white cloth. "I was just in the bathroom."

Great. Now she hadn't wasted her trip.

The guy canted his head at her Civic. "So what's wrong with your car?"

"Nothing." Although if Hutch were here with her, he'd definitely disagree. "My name is Sam Cosi. I'm a private investigator and I'd like to ask you a few questions . . ." She trailed off, intentionally fishing for his name.

"Okay," the guy said, clearly missing her prompt. "What do you wanna know?"

God, please make this go smoothly. She didn't have the patience after her road rage had been sparked. "There was a car you worked on about a week back . . ." As she started describing Matthew's car, the man shook his head.

"Sorry, I don't remember that car coming in."

"Maybe you'll remember his owner then. His name is Matthew Hewitt. I hear he was a regular here."

Again, the guy shook his head.

"Wait." Sam pulled out her phone and Googled Matthew Hewitt. Several images of him appeared on her screen. "This guy," she said, pointing at the picture.

"Hmm. Sorry, but I don't remember working on his car."

Sam pulled the invoice from her bag. "Is this not one of your invoices?"

"Let me see that." Taking the paper from her, he examined it closely before he said, "Oh yeah, yeah! I remember him now."

Relief spread through her. "So you worked on this car?"

"Yeah. My name is Diego Garcia." He held out a hand and Sam shook it.

"Okay, Mr. Garcia. Can you tell me what you did to it?"

"I just did what he asked me to do. Oil change. I checked steering and suspension. You know, that kind of thing."

"What about the brakes?"

"What about them?"

"Did you do anything to them?"

Garcia pointed a finger at the paper she held in her hands. "Well, it says here that they were serviced, so yeah."

"Okay, can you tell me if anything was off about his brakes when he brought it in?"

Garcia shook his head. "No. I don't remember." *Oh man, she was going nowhere with this guy!*

"Nothing?" she pushed. "You can't tell me anything else that was wrong with the car?" A headache was started to form and she knew it would only get worse.

Sam wasn't the only one who was getting impatient either. Garcia glanced over her shoulder at the other two men waiting behind her. "Sorry, lady, but I have customers waiting. Do you want to tell me what this is all about?"

"I'm investigating Matthew Hewitt's accident. He lost control of his car because the brakes weren't working properly."

Garcia's eyes widened with surprise. *"An accident? Is he dead?"*

"No, he's not dead, but he did get banged up pretty badly."

"Oh shit."

Oh shit, indeed. "So that's why I'm here. I'd like to know what happened."

"Wait. You think *I killed him?*" Garcia suddenly looked panicked. It was a nice change from his confused expression earlier. Maybe if she instilled some more fear into him, he'd tell her what she wanted to know.

"I didn't say that, so calm down. I'm just asking some questions."

"But you wouldn't be here if you didn't think I had something to do with the accident! I'm telling you, I didn't touch the brakes!" he wailed.

Sam immediately called on his slip. "But you said you did."

Garcia's face pinched together. "What?"

"A second ago, you just said that you did an oil change, checked steering, suspension, and his brakes."

His hand came up to scratch his balding head. "Then yeah. Yeah, I did."

"Which is it, Mr. Garcia?" Sam didn't appreciate being dicked around. "Did you or did you not touch the brakes?"

"I did," he finally said. "But I didn't do anything other than what he wanted."

What he wanted or what he deserved? Sam took in the mechanic's appearance. He was shorter than her, probably topping out at five-seven. His golden skin reminded her of sunshine and sand, but she couldn't tell if she genuinely confused the man or if it was all an act. She had to proceed with caution with this one. "Do you have a grudge against Matthew Hewitt or do you have any beef with him or anyone in his family?"

"No! Why would I? He's a nice guy and he pays well." Sam arched a brow at this. She might believe that he paid well but as far as she was concerned, Matthew was only nice to Maison.

"You know, Mr. Garcia, I'm really good at telling when people are lying." And she had a feeling that this guy was hiding something.

"I'm not lying!"

"Hey! Is this lady bothering you?" Sam turned to one of the waiting customers. His gaze flipped back and forth between her and Garcia, who clearly looked rattled by their conversation. Sam pierced Garcia with a look.

"No, it's fine," Garcia said quickly. "We're fine. I'll be right with you, sir."

She took a step back and crossed her arms over her chest. "Suppose you didn't do anything wrong. Then how come the cops are saying that someone messed with the brakes?"

"I told you, I don't know!"

"Would a person have had to know a lot about cars to be able to do something like this?"

"Look, lady, I'm not talking to you anymore. I've got work to do. Customers are waiting."

Sam cursed as Garcia walked away. With them around, she wouldn't be able to push him anymore. Plus, her head was pounding so hard, she felt like someone was trying to pry it open with a metal bar. She knew she'd lost any chance of getting more answers when Garcia crossed the garage and started talking to the other customers.

Gritting her teeth, Sam made sure she had the invoice back in her possession before she pulled out one of her business cards and held it out to Garcia. "I'm sorry I jumped on you like that, but a man was hurt. I just want to know what happened that night. If you feel like talking, give me a call."

The guy didn't look at her so Sam left her card on the nearest table, hoping that she hadn't just burned the only bridge that might help her figure out how Matthew's brakes had malfunctioned that night.

NINE

HUNTER HAD CALLED INTO THE OFFICE AND TOLD Maison that he'd be a little late this morning. He wanted to make sure Owen wasn't actually sick from the night before and, to be honest, he was going to take Sam's advice and take a few hours for himself.

He should've felt guilty from keeping Owen home from school, but after the day they'd both had, maybe spending more time with him would be a good thing. If he was tired, then he couldn't imagine what it would be like for Owen.

Hunter stood in the park now, watching on as Owen played with some other kids. He was happy to see him smiling and laughing again. He had no idea what had caused his tantrum yesterday but he was glad to see that the kid was enjoying himself now.

Hopefully, within the next few days, his father would be able to come back home too. Though he didn't want to admit it, he actually missed his offhanded comments and constant pestering. And if he did come home, that meant his days would be cut short at Gleam and he could once again go back to his life as a single dad.

And yet he still worried about his father and his family. The police still hadn't figured out what happened that rainy evening, and since Matthew wasn't actually killed in the accident, the investigation wasn't a top priority. He'd suspected it would take some time before any progress was made. And that was why he was so happy to have Sam looking into things for him.

Without even thinking about it, Hunter pulled his phone out and called her. He wanted to check in with how things had gone at the garage. But also, he just really wanted to hear her voice again.

"Hunter, what a surprise," Sam drawled when she picked up. He liked the smile in her voice. Was she happy that he'd called?

"Can you talk?" He could hear cars beeping in the background. "I just wanted to check in on how things went at the garage."

Instead of hitting him with updates though, Sam asked, "Where are you?"

"Uh, I'm at a park. Why?" Could she hear the kids yelling in the background?

"Which one?"

After he told her, Sam surprised him by saying, "I'm close by. If you want, I can come over there and we can talk in person."

"Ah, sure. That sounds great."

"Cool. I'll be there in five."

Wow. She was coming to see him.

Pleased by how that went, Hunter hung up and checked on Owen. He was now by the swings, watching as another kid went back and forth in the air with increasing speed. Seeing the smile on his face was totally worth the extra hours he'd no doubt have to work later.

About fifteen minutes later, he caught sight of Sam approaching. Once again she was wearing all black. Her hair was pulled back into a sleek ponytail and her lips were covered in a bright shade of red lipstick. *Wow, she looked smokin'.* In her hands, Sam carried two cups of steaming hot coffee. "Hey," he said once she was by his side.

"Hello. This is for you." Sam handed him a coffee.

"Thank you."

Sam smiled at him and he felt his chest constrict. "I didn't know how you took it so I brought some cream and sugar just in case." She pulled out several little packets from her pocket and handed it to him.

"Thanks. But black is fine."

She rolled her eyes at him. "I should've figured." When she took a sip of her own coffee, she let out a long groan. Hunter arched a brow at her.

"First cup of the day?"

"No. I had one earlier this morning but I have this massive headache that won't go away."

"Need some ibuprofen?"

"Thanks, but I have my own." She placed her purse in her lap and started digging through it. "Hallelujah," she said as she popped two in her mouth and chased it with the coffee.

"Bad morning, huh?"

"You have no idea." She pinned him with a look. "You two playing hooky?"

He laughed. "Not exactly. I'm taking what you said yesterday into consideration."

"So your idea of relaxation is spending time in the hot sun with a bunch of screaming kids?"

He laughed again. "Well, when you put it that way, it doesn't sound too good. I just wanted to pretend that I didn't have a million things to do and just spend time with Owen again."

"How is he?"

"Better, I think. I don't know. It's hard to tell with him. One moment he's fine and the next he's turned into Justin Bieber on an acid trip."

Sam laughed. "Just wait until he gets older."

He groaned loudly. "I don't even want to think about that! Did you check out the garage? Were you able to find out anything?"

Sam took a sip of her coffee and made an inelegant snort. "Mr. Garcia is quite the character."

"Yeah? Care to elaborate?"

"Well, he seemed totally fine at first, but when I told him why I was there, he started contradicting himself." He realized she was frowning. "He first said that he worked on the brakes, then he said he didn't."

"But on the invoice, it said—"

"I know. It seemed like he couldn't remember working on the car at all."

"Really? But my dad's been going to him for years."

"I know, so I thought that was a little suspicious."

"You thinking he could've done it?" he asked.

"I can't say but something is off about him. I don't know if he's really that clueless or if he's trying to hide something."

"Well, if he is behind it, the bastard's going to pay." No one was allowed to mess with his family.

Sam glanced over at him and he suddenly felt self-conscious. "I have a question for you. You don't have to answer it," she added hastily. "But I'm curious."

"What do you want to know?"

"Why did you take the job at Gleam? Hutch told me you never wanted it."

He let out a long sigh. He figured a lot of people wanted to know the same thing but he'd refused to speak to them about it. But he found that he couldn't refuse Sam. "No. I had other dreams," he admitted.

"Football, right?"

"Yeah, football. I realized things had to change after I couldn't play anymore."

"I'm sorry to hear that." There was a tinge of sadness in her tone. Hunter wondered if Sam could really understand what it was like to have something you loved, something you built your entire life on and have it taken away from you.

And then he remembered that she had. Hutch had told him that he'd joined the Army because of her. That it had been her dream since she was a little girl but she hadn't been able to pass the tests. He remembered Hutch saying that it had broken her.

He turned to her, taking in her red lips and creamy skin. "Why do you think he told me those things about Clive?"

"You mean your dad?"

When he nodded, Sam shook her head. "I really don't know. Has he said anything else since then?"

"I haven't gone to see him," he said with heavy guilt. "Been busy with Gleam and Owen."

Sam nodded in understanding. But did she though? Could she understand how he felt like he was being pulled two different ways between what he wanted for himself and the obligations he had for his family?

When silence filled the space between them, she said, "Hey, Hunter?"

"Yeah?"

"What's going on between us?"

Heat filled his face. The truth was, he had no idea. "I don't know," he answered honestly. "But I do know that I enjoy spending time with you."

He also knew that he liked her, but he wasn't sure if he should reveal that to her now, especially since he had no idea how she felt for him.

Sam was on the verge of saying something when her phone rang. She shot him an apologetic look. "Oh no," she said when she glanced down at the screen.

"What is it?"

"It's my mother."

"Go ahead and take it." It might be important. But by the expression on Sam's face, she looked annoyed by the interruption.

"Hey, Mom. I'm kind of busy right now."

"So how did the date with Lorenzo go?" her mother asked.

Lorenzo? Who the hell was that? Oh, right. "It was okay. But I don't think I'm interested."

"What do you mean? He's a very nice boy!"

Sam stood abruptly, covering her phone's mouthpiece with her hand. "I'm so sorry, I'll be just a moment," she said to him.

"No problem." Except Hunter really wanted to hear more of the conversation. *Who the hell was this Lorenzo guy?*

But all traces of his jealously were dashed away when the sudden high-pitched scream of a child had him bolting up from his seat. "What the hell was that?"

Sam whipped around, glancing back at him before they both bolted toward the sound. Other parents were running toward the swings too, concerned as well. What the hell happened? Was one of the kids hurt? Was Owen?

He was surprised to find two kids standing by the swings. One of them was being pulled away into the arms of a woman who he supposed was the kid's mother. The other kid was Owen. "What happened?" he asked as he came to stand by his son. He was surprised to find Sam right behind him, not at all panicking and out of breath like he was.

One of the other parents was yelling at Owen. "Where are

your parents? I can't believe they'd just leave you out here like this!"

"I'm right here. What's going on?"

The woman swung her enraged glare at him. "*You're* his father?"

"I just said I was." He had no idea why she was being so rude, but he didn't have to be considerate when she clearly wasn't going to be.

The woman flung an accusing finger at Owen who flinched like he'd been hit. "Your son here doesn't know what waiting your turn means! He just tried ripping out my kid's hair!"

What?

Hunter swung his shocked face at Owen and dropped down beside him. "Owen, is this true? Owen," he repeated when he didn't reply. "Did you pull his hair?"

When his kid continued to ignore him, Hunter sighed. He rose again, turning back to the woman. "I'm sorry. I don't know what's gotten into him. He's been acting out lately and I'm still trying to figure it out."

"You should keep a better watch on him," the woman spat. "A firm hand will always keep children in line. Maybe you should think about disciplining your child so he learns a thing or two about hurting others!" With her head held high, she turned, pushing past the gathered crowd.

What the fuck? He'd been polite and apologized and she was throwing it back in his face? Hunter was fuming now. While he was more than ready to admit that Owen had done something wrong, having this stranger lecture him on how to discipline his son made him beyond furious.

"Teach your kid some manners," another woman snarled. Hunter turned, readying to defend himself but he was surprised to see that the woman was addressing Sam.

"The kid is sorry, okay?" Sam said, not at all intimidated by being ganged up on. "I'm sure his father will come up with a suitable way to discipline his son." Hunter opened his mouth to say that she didn't need to stand up for him but Sam went on without hesitation. "So you can all go back to your minivans and drive back to your cul-de-sacs. I'm sure an episode of Rachel Ray will cheer you right back up and you'll forget all about today's little mishap." If he weren't so irritated by what happened, Hunter would've laughed at the other women's expressions. "Go on now." She made shooing motions with her hands. "Don't you have some homework to do?"

Now he did laugh out loud. Wow, no one had ever done that for him before. And he especially loved that she was standing up for his kid.

In a huff, the last woman walked off, obviously pissed off.

When Sam turned back to him, her face was bright and smug. "I can't believe you just did that!" he yelled, both impressed and overjoyed.

"They were the ones being rude first. I'll admit, the kid made a mistake, but he's just a kid, you know?" Sam stared down at Owen and ruffled his hair affectionately. "Hey, little guy, remember me?"

Owen grinned up at her.

"So," Sam started, "how are we going to do this?"

We? he thought. But before Hunter could ask what she meant, Sam dropped down to her knees so that she was level with his son. "You want to tell me why you pulled that boy's hair?"

Intrigued, Hunter listened on. "It was *my* turn," Owen said angrily. "He already went on *three times!*"

Sam shot him a look. "Okay," she said, voice still calm. "But even if that was the case, I don't think pulling his hair was a nice way to approach things. What do you think you should have done instead?"

Owen's mouth twisted like he was thinking hard and also trying hard not to cry. "I don't know," he said finally.

While he appreciated everything that Sam had done for them, it was time for him to step in. "Owen, what you did was wrong," he started. "First of all, we don't *ever* pull someone else's hair, got it?" He waited for the kid to nod in understanding. "And secondly, if it wasn't his turn, you should have told him politely. We don't react with violence like that, okay?"

"Okay."

"What do you think is suitable punishment?" he asked Sam.

Sam didn't miss a beat. "No TV for a week?"

"What?" Owen exclaimed. "No!"

"Sounds good to me," he agreed. Owen loved TV. "But we're also not coming to the park in that time either." That would teach him a lesson.

Sam raised an eyebrow at this, but she didn't disagree. Owen, however, looked like he *totally* disagreed with the way he was shaking his head. "But, Dad!" he argued.

Hunter hugged him close. "Sorry, Owen, but you have to learn. Hopefully this won't happen again. Thanks for your help," he said when he turned back to Sam.

"No problem. Pisses me off to see them all ganging up on a kid like that. Probably scared him senseless."

"Yeah." He ran his hand over the top of Owen's head. "I just wish I knew what was going on with him . . ."

"Maybe it's stress?" Sam suggested.

"Could be."

A lot had changed in their lives. Since the divorce, he felt like they were walking on moving ground. And with his father's accident and now this new job, the changes were still coming.

"Just take it one day at a time."

"Yeah. It can still get a little overwhelming at times," he admitted.

"Well, like I said yesterday, I'm happy to help in any way that I can. Or what about Hutch or Dacey? Would they be able to help you out?"

"They're great. But sometimes I can't help but wonder what else is missing from his life that I can't give him." He didn't want to say it. But seeing Sam out there, dishing it right back out because someone had been rude to his son, made him wonder if having someone else around would better help Owen. Maybe his son needed someone who could be a mother figure to him because, hell, he knew he couldn't do it.

But no, he couldn't unload that kind of responsibility on Sam. She already had a lot on her plate.

"We'd better get home," he told Owen. "Do you want to join us for lunch?" After a quick bite, he'd have to go into the office.

Sam smiled sweetly at him. "Thanks, but no, thanks."

"Okay. Will I see you around again?"

"Absolutely." To his surprise, Sam reached up on her tiptoes and placed a small kiss on his cheek. He looked at her in confusion.

Sam rolled her eyes at him. "Don't look so shocked. If you didn't realize I like you already, then maybe I need a lesson in romance." Her smile disappeared, turning shy. "I'm sorry for my mother's interruption, but I was going to say that I'd like to spend more time with you when you have the time. Is that cool?"

His brain was slow to comprehend because he was pretty sure that all his blood was now rushing toward his lower body.

His reaction must've shown on his face because Sam laughed. "Okay. I'll let you think about it." She waved as she backed away from him.

He suddenly found his voice. "Where are you going?"

"I've got some work to do, but maybe I'll call you later?"

Hunter grinned. "Yeah, I'd like that."

With another wave, Sam turned around and started back where she'd come from. He watched her until she slid back into her car.

Holy shit, he thought when she was gone. *Sam Cosi had kissed him!*

TEN

Later that evening, Sam sat at her dinner table after fixing up a meal for one and called her mother back. Rosanna had been entirely miffed that she'd hung up on her earlier, so Sam braced herself for a lashing. Of course she was back on the topic of her sister's wedding and her "sadly single status."

As her mother blabbered on, Sam jabbed her fork into her mashed potatoes. What did it matter anyway? Since when had being in a relationship guaranteed success in life? For thirty years she'd made it on her own without a man. Why did that suddenly have to change once she hit thirty-one?

And why couldn't she just show up alone and have her mother be content with it? Her focus should be on Serena, not her. Sam honestly didn't care what the rest of her family thought of her. She'd rather be left alone.

Her phone beeped and Sam rejoiced at the sight of her sister's name on the screen. "Mom, Serena is on the other line. I'll call you back." She switched lines without even waiting for a response. "God, your mother is driving me crazy!"

"You?" Serena shot back. "She's been bugging me nonstop every day! What's she on your ass for?"

Sam sighed. "She wants me to find a date for the wedding."

"She's matchmaking?"

"She has been for months! Why did you have to get engaged? You could've saved me a lot of trouble."

She could hear the smile in her sister's voice. "Sorry. I'll call the wedding off then."

"Perfect," she teased back and then sighed again. "I can't handle all this extra pressure. I'm too busy to worry about that kind of stuff. Do you mind talking to her for me?"

"What good will that do? She has always listened to you more."

"Not on this. I just don't know why she's so adamant about me finding a guy."

"I guess she just wants to show others that you're not alone."

"Being alone is what I prefer," she said, although that wasn't entirely true. Sam thought of Hunter and of his surprised expression when she'd kissed him. She still didn't know why she'd done that. It had been a complete impulsive reaction, but she didn't regret it.

She meant what she'd said about enjoying spending time with him and Owen. But there was no way she'd have the guts to ask Hunter to come with her to the wedding. If worse came to worst, she'd take Deacon and hoped that he didn't make a fool of himself in front of everyone.

"Ugh. Forget about it. How is the rest of the wedding going?"

As Serena fell into a tirade all about her caterer, Sam finished her dinner. "Don't worry, everything will be okay. Meanwhile, will you tell Mom to back off?"

"I'll see what I can do."

"Thank you."

"Love you."

"Love you, too."

After hanging up, Sam washed the dishes and did a quick tidy of the kitchen. Exhausted from the day, she settled into the couch and turned on the TV, excited to be diving back into her favorite crime drama. But when the opening scene was of a car accident, her mind trailed back to Hunter.

Oh God. She'd kissed him. Did he like it? She certainly had. Once her lips had met his stubble, an electric shock had gone through her. He'd smelled so good, like sandalwood and leather, that she wanted to bury her nose into his neck. She wanted to kiss him more, to forget about all that was happening and simply enjoy fiery, crackling energy that sparked since the first time they'd laid eyes on each other.

But she still wasn't sure where Hunter stood in all this. Did he feel the chemistry between them too? And if so, why hadn't he acted on it? She knew from Hutch that Hunter had gathered a lot of attention from many women in the past. He was the kind of guy who made pleasure a priority; "a master of anticipation" as Hutch had called him. Did that mean he was a patient lover? Or did he like it rough and dirty, but still made sure the woman was enjoying herself?

No wonder Hutch was jealous of his brother. He sounded like heaven. But Sam wasn't going to be able to know more until she figured out this case. With that sobering reminder, she picked up her phone and called Deacon.

He answered on the second ring. "Is this some booty call?" Sounds of music and chatter echoed in the background and she wondered if he was at a club or a bar.

"What the hell are you talking about?"

"Most people who call me at this time are looking to hook up."

Sam smiled at the hopeful tone of his voice. "You wish and it's only ten o'clock. I was just calling for an update."

"Bummer," he muttered.

"So did you see Brian?"

"Yup."

"And?"

"I'm not sure he's our guy." As he explained how he'd checked out his alibi and he'd come out clean, Sam sighed.

"Really? So if not him, then who?"

"Well, we discovered something else . . ."

"What?"

"There was some brake fluid on Clive's car. We all thought it was just rain that night but it's very visible now."

"Brake fluid? So it really was him. *Oh my God,*" she breathed.

"Yeah. It sucks."

"Wait. Have you told Hunter this already?"

"Not yet. It's late and I was thinking of just calling him in the morning."

Sam nodded. A phone call would likely wake Owen up. "So this was really a simple case of a business partner wanting more of his share?"

"Yup."

For whatever reason, she wasn't as happy as she should be. Deacon realized this because he said, "Come on, Sam. This is a good thing."

It *was* a good thing. Deacon had figured it out. She forced herself to smile. "You're right. It is a good thing."

"So that's it? That's all you wanted to talk to me about?"

"Yeah. Good night, Deacon."

"Fine," he grumbled. "But one day you'll realize that you want me."

Sam smiled wide now. "Maybe but I wouldn't hold your breath for it." She hung up on him before he could respond.

ELEVEN

DESPITE THE GOOD NEWS, SAM SPENT THE ENTIRE night tossing and turning in bed. By early morning, she'd totally given up on trying to sleep and opted for staring at her ceiling instead. She should be happy. Deacon and the Moonrise Beach Police Department had the evidence to prove that Clive Davenport had done it. But something still bothered her about it all.

If it had been him, how had he found the time to do something to the brakes if he was with Matthew the entire time? Surely Hunter's father would've realized that something was up if his friend had disappeared.

Something wasn't adding up, but since she had limited knowledge on brake mechanics, she had no idea if her gut was just playing with her or if she was just being silly. But her instincts had never steered her wrong before so as soon as the sun was up, Sam was out of bed and back on the road.

This time traffic wasn't so bad so she reached Auto Fix in thirty minutes. "You again?" Garcia said when he saw her. "What the hell are you doing here?"

Determined not to have a repeat of the last time she was here, Sam smiled. She'd stopped at a nearby coffeehouse and bought two cups of coffee. She handed one to Garcia now. But the guy stared at it like it was a diseased animal. "Take it," she snapped. "I didn't poison it if that's what you're worried about."

She was glad when Garcia took the cup from her and

took a sip. It was still early and no one else was around yet. It was the perfect opportunity to get some answers out of Garcia. "I'm sorry for the way I acted the last time I was here. I had a headache and my patience was wearing thin. I took it out on you."

Garcia looked surprised by her words but he didn't say anything so Sam continued, "The police are going to arrest someone today. Since you said you worked on the brakes when Matthew brought his car in, could you maybe explain to me how one would go about tampering with someone's brakes?" Garcia looked like she'd just asked him to jump off a cliff. "Is it messy?" she asked, thinking of the spilled brake fluid that Deacon had found.

"It can be if you don't know what you're doing."

Sam gave him a look that hopefully conveyed that she wanted him to continue. After a sigh, Garcia said, "You said that he was driving when the accident happened?"

"Yes." That was what she'd been told. Matthew had swerved to avoid hitting something and probably realized then that something was wrong with his brakes.

"Then it sounds like whoever did it knew what they were doing."

"Yeah?" How did Clive know how to do it? He didn't strike her as a man who would get down on his hands and knees very much.

Garcia nodded. "If he was able to drive it, it means that the person probably made a hole small enough that no one would notice. It would still work for a while." And the rain may have also helped disguise any fluid that may have leaked.

"The person would've needed to time it correctly or it would've been noticeable right away. I checked out my files after you left, just to make sure I wasn't getting mixed up. You showing up out of the blue threw me for a loop," he admitted. "But you'll see on your invoice as well that he saw me *a week* before the accident. That would be too much time."

Sam found it funny that she was still trying to prove his innocence. "What if you did it while his car was in Clive's driveway?"

Garcia shook his head. "I don't personally know Clive so I don't know where he lives. And I also don't have a reason to kill Matthew. He's a customer."

Sam was starting to feel bad for the guy. She'd come here, guns blazing, pointing fingers and pushing him into a corner, hoping that he'd admit to a crime he hadn't committed. She'd been in the wrong and she'd known it. That was why she was here. Her subconscious felt guilty.

She guessed Deacon was right. Clive really was the one behind it all since Garcia didn't have a motive.

"Again, I'm sorry about how I acted the other day. I was rude."

Garcia grinned at her. "It's all right. I wasn't exactly ac-commodating either. So who are the cops arresting?" he asked.

"You'll find out soon." She stood, ignoring his expression of shock and headed for her car. She turned back only to say, "Thanks for answering my questions." She lifted her cup up in the air. "Cheers."

"You suck, lady!" Garcia called out after her.

"Don't call me *lady*," she gritted as she peeled out of the lot.

"Hey, man. Want to go for drinks again tonight?" A hand squeezed his shoulder and Deacon Thorpe turned around in his desk to meet the eyes of his friend Juliana Michaels.

Whereas his eyes were glassy with lack of sleep, her blue eyes pierced into him like lasers.

"I probably shouldn't." He was still feeling hung over from last night's events and although he'd been able to party for an entire week when he was in college, he recovered more slowly now at thirty-three.

Juliana shrugged. "Fine. Suit yourself. But you're going to miss out on a good time."

Deacon grinned. Oh, he knew he would. Last night they'd indulged in some early celebration. For a long time they'd suspected Clive Davenport to be behind Matthew Hewitt's accident, but there hadn't been any evidence to prove it. Now that they did have something, he was so eager to take the guy in. It would be another win for him.

While he often flirted and joked, there was only one thing he took seriously. His career had always been precious to him and he'd worked very hard to get where he was in the department. Not only had he earned the respect of his colleagues but those above him liked him as well. As long as he kept this position there would be no complaints from him.

"You ready to go now?"

"Sure, let me just give Hunter a call." He would be ecstatic and hopefully relieved to put this all to rest. Unlike Sam who seemed less thrilled than he expected her to be when he'd told her the news.

Although Sam wasn't a cop like he was, she was the smartest person he knew and he liked using her investigating skills to his advantage. He liked to tease her and flirt with her, but he knew it was all in good fun. If he really wanted her to be his, he'd have made it known more clearly.

When Hunter picked up his phone and he explained what he was about to do, he smiled at the relief in Hunter's voice. "Thank you," his friend said.

Deacon could only nod in answer. "I'll talk to you later."

"Okay, bye."

"Bye." Hanging up, he turned to Juliana again. She grinned at him from her perch at his desk. "You ready?" he asked.

Juliana pulled out her handcuffs. "Honey, I was born ready."

TWELVE

LTHOUGH SHE HAD OTHER WORK THAT NEEDED HER attention, Sam headed straight for Gleam Enterprises after leaving Auto Fix. But traffic had picked up and by the time she arrived and made it up to Hunter's floor, she realized that it was lunchtime. "Shit." *What was she going to do now? Go back to her office?*

"Hey, Sam, how's it going?"

She turned to find Maison standing behind her. "Uh, hey, Maison." She felt foolish for standing there in the middle of the hallway while everyone else moved past her to go to the elevators.

"Are you here to see Hunter?" Maison asked.

"Yeah." She hesitated. "Is he around?" She really needed to get into the habit of calling in. Though they were friends, she knew he was too busy of a man for her to just walk in when she wanted.

"He's inside his office. I don't think he'll mind if you go in."

"Thanks." As she moved past the other woman, she paused. "Do you guys know? Did Deacon call?"

Maison nodded. Her smile morphed into a frown. "Yeah, he just did. I can't believe it."

Sam felt bad for the woman. From the very beginning she'd been against the idea of Clive being behind it all, but sometimes people surprised us.

"It'll be okay." And hopefully, Gleam Enterprises could still come back from this.

Maison nodded sullenly. "At least the Happa-Hewitts can relax now, knowing the worst has passed."

"Yes," she agreed.

It hit her then that there would be no reason for her to come and see Hunter anymore. Now that they'd found out who was behind the accident, she could move onto another case.

Normally, an achievement like this would make her happy. But Sam realized that she would miss talking to Hunter.

As if knowing she was thinking about him, the doors to the glass office opened and Hunter stepped out. His dark gaze immediately latched onto her and he seemed surprised to see her. "Sam," he breathed. "What are you doing here?"

"I wanted to talk to you but I realize I'm interfering with your lunch. I'll wait until you've come back."

"Don't be silly. You can come have lunch with me."

"What?" *Have lunch with Hunter?* Her face flushed red. "I—I don't think—"

"Maison, would you like to join us?"

"No, thanks," Maison chimed, back to her normal sweet self. "Hutch is coming and we're going out too."

Hunter made a face. "I see enough of his face at home. Far be it for me to want to see his face again so soon."

Maison laughed, but Sam was still recovering. Hunter then turned to her. "I guess it's just you and me then." He flashed her a dazzling smile that didn't help her already panicked state.

When she didn't say anything, his eyes narrowed and she could feel his gaze scanning over her. To her surprise, he reached out, brushing his finger against her cheek. "Sam, are you okay? You look a little pale."

"I'm fine," she lied.

His brows drew together and his mouth formed a frown. "Have you been up all night?" he asked.

God, did she look that bad? Surprising her further, Hunter took her hand. "Come on, let's feed you before you collapse."

"But—" She glanced frantically back at Maison, but the other woman wasn't aware of her distress. She simply smiled and waved them off.

Sam tried to pull back as they reached the elevators. "Where are we going?"

Hunter shot a grin at her. "It's a surprise."

Hunter was glad that she'd come with him. After getting the call from Deacon and the Moonrise Beach Police Department, he was sure the rest of his day was going to crap. But despite the endless meetings he'd have to endure later, he was excited now that Sam was here. While she still looked gorgeous in her signature ripped jeans and curve-hugging tank top, her skin looked paler than usual.

His protective nature immediately rose to the surface and he found himself reaching for her. Her skin was soft. Smooth as silk, and he wondered what the rest of her body would feel like if he ran his hands over it.

He was trying to act casual, but inside his chest, his heart was rattling against his ribs, trying to leap out. After she'd kissed him in the park, there was no going back for him.

At first he'd wanted to go slow, to take his time like he always did with everything else in his life. But one kiss from Sam had turned him into a blazing inferno and he wanted more. Call him greedy but he wasn't about to let her regret kissing him now.

After Deacon's call earlier, he'd fallen into a panic, and although what his friend was telling him should make him happy, he couldn't help but think what this would mean for Gleam.

When the elevator doors opened, Hunter glanced over

his shoulder at Sam. He was glad to see that she was still with him but something was off about her. Gone was the confident woman he knew. Now she seemed to be replaced with someone as shy as his new assistant.

"How do you feel about sushi?" he asked as they both stepped into the elevator cab together.

The doors closed and Sam looked up at him. "I love sushi."

Great. He knew a place nearby that was amazing. Once the doors closed, Hunter pulled her close. He heard her gasp of surprise but she didn't push him away. A smirk quirked his lips as he felt her grip the end of his tie. "Hunter," she whispered against his chest. "Are you—"

"I'm okay." He loved that she was worried about him. He figured that was why she'd come. Deacon must've told her about what he was going to do and she wanted to make sure that he wasn't losing his head over it. "Are you?"

This time she did pull back, but only far enough so that she could look up at him. "I'm a little tired," she admitted, "but I wanted to see you."

He clutched her tighter. "I'm glad you came."

When the doors opened again, he took her hand and they walked the three-minute walk to the restaurant.

Sushi Kiss was packed when they arrived and it took them another five minutes for them to get a table. By then, Hunter was ravenous. They ordered quickly and ate in comfortable silence for a few minutes before Hunter set his miso soup down.

The color was coming back into Sam's face and she smiled up at him when she caught him looking. "You look very beautiful," he said.

A pink flush appeared high on her cheeks and he chuckled. Sam fussed with her hair, looking suddenly shy and girly. "I don't know what it is about you but you make me feel things that no other man has."

A wolfish smile spread over his lips. He didn't want to sound cocky or so sure of himself but he liked Sam's straightforwardness. It cut through the unnecessary emotions and gave them something solid to build on. "I'll admit, I hadn't expected this. But I had a feeling you liked me. I intended to wait, perhaps after all this was over, but I don't think I can."

Sam leaned closer into the table. "Well, technically, as of today, it is over." They'd found out what had happened to his father and now they could rest easy that they were all safe now.

"Then I guess there's nothing else holding me back," he said.

That got the reaction he'd wanted. Sam smiled brilliantly, and it took all his strength not to get out of his seat and kiss her.

"Do you think things will change now? At Gleam, I mean?"

"Probably." He couldn't see how they could go back to how it'd been before. And once his father returned, he doubted he'd want Clive working with him again.

Sam reached over the table and wrapped her hand around his. It was so much smaller than his, so much more delicate, but he knew that Sam was capable of so many amazing things. He didn't think the Moonrise Beach Police Department would've figured it out without her help. He brought her hand to his lips. "Thank you," he whispered. "Thank you for helping me protect my family." He kissed her hand then, letting his gaze penetrate deep. He wanted her to know how much he felt for her, how much he felt indebted for all that she'd done for him and his family.

Sam pulled her hand away, suddenly embarrassed. "Hunter," she whispered. "You're making me feel nervous."

He felt nervous too. No, more like anxious. Now that they'd formed solid ground together, he wanted to run with it. "Do you want to go out with me?" By her expression, she looked surprised. "I mean like on a real date."

A smile curled her lips. "You mean you're actually going to take some time for yourself?" she teased.

"For you I will. Come on, it'll be nice. We'll finally get to know each other better." After hearing about her for years from Hutch, he was desperate to know more about this wonderful woman.

"How's Owen doing?" Sam asked him instead.

What? Hunter had to blink to realize that she'd completely dodged his question. Owen? "Um, he's okay." Sam nodded but she didn't say anything. "So you're just going to leave me hanging and not answer my question?"

She shot him a shy smile. "I don't really date much," she admitted.

He felt his heart clench in his chest. "So is that a no?"

"I didn't say that."

Phew. "So then what are you saying?"

"I just want to warn you."

"Warn me about what? Are you a bad date or something?"

"Something like that."

He reached over and grabbed a hold of her hand again. That was when he realized that she was shaking. Concern filled him and he made sure she was looking him in the eyes when he said, "You lit up my world with that one kiss, Sam. And it made me realize that I was letting life pass me by. I had spent so much of my time living for others that I'd forgotten what it felt like to have something solely for me. You're that one thing for me, Sam. You're what I want."

Sam sat there in silence, looking shocked by the raw emotion of his words. He was clutching her hand like a lifeline, fearing that she would slip away now that he'd told her everything.

But instead of pulling away, Sam's shaking stopped and she smiled at him. "You're going to regret saying that."

"I am?"

"Yes. If we start dating, you're going to have to meet my family eventually, and once you do, you're going to be running the other way."

Hunter grinned. Her family? How bad could they be? "We'll see about that."

THIRTEEN

S AM DIDN'T REALIZE THAT IN GOING TO SEE HUNTER that she'd somehow end up with a date, but she had. She'd specifically asked that they take it slow though. All this was so out of her element that it felt a bit like a dream. After some convincing on his part, they'd agreed to go out this weekend. And for the first time in a long time, Sam found herself actually excited to go out with someone.

She was tempted to call her mother, but then figured what was the point? She'd only riddle her with questions about him and Sam wasn't sure she was ready to divulge the details just yet. She wanted to savor this moment and get it right. If all went well tonight, maybe she'd ask him if he'd like to be her date for Serena's wedding.

When Hunter picked her up, Sam was relieved to see that he'd chosen to take her to a steakhouse and bar instead of some place fancy. The guys her mother usually set her up with always tried to impress her by throwing money around. It was clear that they had no idea what actually interested her because fancy food and dim lighting weren't her cup of tea. Maybe that was why she'd been single all this time . . . It was because every other male treated her like how they expected a woman to be like. No one actually took the time to try and understand *her*.

No one but Hunter.

Hunter glanced over at her. "You're smiling. Does that mean I picked a good place?"

"Yes, actually. I'm a bit surprised. Usually guys take women to really fancy places like Sage & Saffron."

"I like it there too but I figured this place was your style."

"It is," she agreed. She loved that he took what she liked into consideration. Although they didn't know each other very well yet, she could tell that Hunter was the kind of guy that paid attention to people.

The corners of his lips tipped up in a boyish smirk. "Also, I may have asked Hutch what you like."

She laughed in a burst. "You're a bit sneaky, aren't you?"

Hunter shrugged like a boy who'd been caught checking out another girl. She found it adorably sexy.

So Hutch knew they were out on a date together. What did he think about it? She hadn't actually told him anything about what was going on with her and Hunter, but would it make things awkward between them now that she was dating his brother?

"Actually, I hadn't meant to tell him," Hunter explained. "But I had to ask him to watch over Owen and you know how Hutch can be when he thinks you're trying to hide something from him."

Oh yeah. She knew all too well of Hutch and his nosiness. He was like a hound dog that wouldn't quit. "I feel bad for Owen," she drawled. "He'll be with him all night."

Hunter grinned. "He'll survive. So what do you feel like eating?"

Picking up the menu, she took a moment to read it over. There were a lot of things she wanted but she'd been craving a burger for a few days now. When she looked up, she caught Hunter staring at her.

Heat crept into her cheeks but Hunter didn't look away as their gazes locked and held. "Stop," she said on a laugh.

"Sorry." But he didn't look sorry at all. That devilish smirk was in place, curling one side of his lips. The urge to kiss him again hit her hard. She still couldn't believe that she was here with him right now. While it wouldn't be such a stretch to see her in a place like this, having Hunter here as her date made everything feel different to her.

"Are you ready to order?"

"Oh!" She didn't realize she'd gotten lost in her own thoughts. Sam hadn't even noticed the waitress arrive and she worried that she might've been rude when she hadn't answered her. "I'll have a burger," she started, listing her choice of side dishes as she was prompted. If Hunter cared about what she ate, he certainly wouldn't have brought her here. She was glad when he'd ordered the same.

"Okay, I'll be right back with your food," the waitress said.

Hunter reached out and grabbed his beer. "I gotta say, it's been a while since I've been out without Owen."

Sam smiled at him, thinking of the little guy. "Missing him already?"

"Yes, but I'm glad I'm here with you."

"Being a father is a tough job."

"Yeah, but it's still the best job."

"What about Gleam? Are you liking it now?" Since Matthew was still recovering, Hunter had to play the part of a billionaire CEO.

"It's definitely growing on me."

She liked hearing that things were going better for him. She'd been so worried about him that she'd done all she could to make sure that he and his family were safe.

"Has Deacon told you anything about Clive?"

Hunter shook his head. She knew that the Moonrise Beach Police Department had taken Clive in for further questioning, but she hadn't heard anything about it apart from what was being revealed in the news. "No." Hunter reached for her hand across the table. "But let's not talk about me. I want to know more about you."

"What do you want to know?"

"What got you into private investigating?"

"Well, it kind of just happened for me," she admitted.

"That's right. You were in the Army with Hutch."

She nodded. "We'd hoped to make it together but I actually didn't make it through training."

"Shit, that must've been hard."

"It was. It crushed me at the time and I had a really hard time accepting it."

"Pardon me for asking but why were you so interested in joining?"

"It'd always been a dream of mine since I was little. I've always been fascinated by it but never understood why it was always men fighting. Why couldn't women do it too? I guess I just wanted to prove myself."

"So after that you came back here?"

"Yes, Moonrise Beach has always been my home. I only got into private investigating after I'd witnessed a crime and was interviewed by the police. Instead of walking away and forgetting about it, I became somewhat of an amateur sleuth while also helping the cops when I could. It turns out I'm pretty good at it. One cop even encouraged me to join the academy but I was too independent for that. I wanted to be my own boss so private investigating seemed like the perfect fit for me. Now I just help him out when I can."

"Let me guess, is this cop Deacon Thorpe?"

Sam grinned. "Yes, it's Deacon." She owed a lot to him for helping her along the way. Helping him solve this case was just her returning the favor.

Hunter leaned into the table, his dark eyes going obsidian. "So have you and Deacon ever . . ."

Oh God! Was he really insinuating—"No, we're strictly friends." And business colleagues when the situation warranted it. "And nothing more. Deacon just likes to flirt but he knows I'm not interested."

Relief spread over Hunter's features. "Good. I'd hate to have to beat him up after all he's done for me and my family." Sam laughed before reaching for her beer. As she polished it off, Hunter asked, "Do you want another one?"

"No. I think I'm done." A flash of disappointment crossed over his features before he could mask it. "Let's go someplace else," she said instead.

"Where?"

"I don't know." She glanced around the bar. She liked the laid-back atmosphere of this place. "Let's just go to another bar or something."

"Okay." Hunter waved a waiter down. Within a few minutes, they were out of the bar, looking for another one. "What about this place?" Hunter suggested.

She looked to where he was pointing. The biker bar that looked a little rough-hewn and dark and she could see several Harleys parked in the front. Something that sounded a lot like live music blared from inside. Grabbing Hunter's hand, she dragged him toward Cooke's Corner. "Let's go!"

The heat of his body against hers permeated through her clothes, heating her instantly. She loved how big he was. Most guys she knew were smaller and didn't make her feel safe in their arms.

As they walked inside together, Sam was hit with the stench of alcohol. Several other rough-looking patrons turned to look at them, but they either didn't care who they were or didn't see them as a threat so they turned back to their own business.

Sam grinned. *Oh yeah, this was so her.*

Hunter slapped a few bills on the bar and ordered a couple more drinks for them. At this point, she was feeling more than a little buzzed but she was just going to roll with it. There was no way she was going to end this so soon.

As they waited for their drinks, Sam allowed her gaze to run down the length of Hunter's long body. It seemed that he'd taken a page from her wardrobe because he was dressed in head to toe black. Black jeans hugged his hips and thick thighs, reminding her of how sturdy he felt against her. The T-shirt he wore exposed his big arms, and Sam noted that she liked the sight of the veins popping out slightly on his forearms. They reminded her of strength and sexiness, adding fuel to her already burning desire for him.

How the hell did this guy manage to look good in both a T-shirt and jeans and a full three-piece suit was beyond her, but there was no way she was going to—

Someone hopped onto the little stage located at the front of the bar and tapped on the mic. "Hello? Does this shit work?"

"It works fine!" called someone from the crowd. Sam looked at Hunter. *Wait a minute. Was she going to sing?*

She got her answer a second later when the woman smiled and pulled out a guitar. As the rest of her band started filing in, Sam grabbed Hunter's hand and led him toward the small crowd. "Hey! What are you—" She quickly wrapped her arms around him. "*Sam.*"

Her eyes flashed with mischief. "Know how to dance?"

Hunter's eyes widened with shock before darkening to obsidian. "If it means being pressed up against you all night, then yeah." Hunter brushed her hair out of her face. "You all right, babe? Are you drunk?"

Her grin widened. "No. I'm just really happy." She hadn't felt this happy in years. Sam had spent so much time trying to prove herself to others that she hadn't realized that she didn't have to try with Hunter.

When he'd come to her to ask for her help, he'd already shown her that he had confidence and trust in her. And yet she'd pushed herself when she didn't have to try and prove herself.

"Good." Hunter brought her closer to him and Sam became well aware of the steel rod pressing against her. He must've known what she was thinking by the look on her face because he said, "Sorry, sweetheart. But that's all because of you."

All for me, she wanted to say but she settled for grinding herself against him. When she was with Hunter, she felt sexy and sweet. Hunter brought the woman out of her and instead of wanting to just wear her boots all the time, she wanted things like heels and frilly things. Was this what her mother had said when she'd told her that one day she'd want something different for herself? Sam still wasn't sure, but even if she switched to wearing heels sometimes, that didn't mean she'd forgotten about who she really was.

Even with the blasting music around them, she could hear Hunter's low groan as they danced. In a bold move, she reached up and dropped her mouth to his neck, licking a quick line up it.

She was rewarded with another low groan before he pulled her tighter against his body. Now, not even a sliver of air separated them.

When she looked up, Sam met eyes swirling with lust. God, she loved this. When was the last time she felt something like this and didn't have to worry about what came in the morning? For the first time in a long time, she could enjoy the company of this very sexy man and do whatever the hell she wanted.

Sam turned, pressing her back to Hunter's front, luxuriating in the feel of his thick arms around her waist. She started to sway to the music, letting her head fall back against his chest as the bright colorful lights of the bar shone down on them.

At her ear, Hunter whispered, "I want you, Sam. I want you so fucking badly, it hurts." The desperation in his voice helped in setting her on fire. She probably wouldn't be able to say no to him if he tried to take her here.

Turning back around, she circled her arms around his neck again. Hunter dipped his head this time, low enough that their mouths were only a couple of inches apart. But he didn't kiss her yet. No, he simply licked his lips, coating them with a wetness that made her want to devour him whole. "What now?" he asked. "Do you want to go to another bar?"

"No. Let's go home." She couldn't wait any longer. She was already burning with her desire for him and nothing but his hands and mouth on her would sate it.

She didn't have to tell him twice. Hunter took her hand and dragged her out of the bar. Sam laughed the whole ride back to her house. She'd never seen a guy act so fast. It was a damned miracle that they didn't maul each other in the streets.

Keys in hand, Sam made sure she was ready so that once the car stopped, they could get right to the good stuff. It was a good thing she was prepared because once she managed to swing the door open, Hunter was on her.

He knocked into her so quickly that they both slammed

into the opposite wall.

"Oh!" she cried as her breath was knocked out of her but there was no pain in her body. Just pleasure. "Hurry!" she begged as she tore at his clothes. "I can't wait!"

"Shh, you'll wake the neighbors." Neighbors? Fuck them. She didn't care. *She needed this.*

As Hunter worked on removing his shirt, Sam went straight for his zipper. "Fuck," he gritted. "You're so hot."

Her? He was the one burning her up. All their talking and dancing had riled her up good and now she felt like she was going to explode if he wasn't inside her soon.

"Please," she begged when she couldn't take it any longer. "I need you inside me."

Hunter didn't waste a second more. He was lifting her and she wrapped her legs around his waist. Power radiated from his body, and for a moment, Sam felt like she weighed no more than a feather by how easily he carried her.

Not many men could make her feel dainty or riled her up to the point where she felt like she was going to burst. Only Hunter did and Sam realized with a start that this was what she'd been missing all this time. With all those other men her mother had been pushing onto her, they'd all lacked that alpha personality that she was naturally drawn to.

She almost wanted to laugh. She'd finally figured out what it was she'd been missing all her life but she'd found it in the one guy she knew she couldn't have. How was that fair?

The shrill sound of a phone ringing had them both freezing in place. "What the hell is that?" Hunter cursed before setting her down gently. She watched as he reached into his back pocket and pulled out his phone. On the screen, Hutch's name flashed. *Shit. Had something happened?*

She saw that he was going to ignore it when she said, "No.

Answer it. He might be calling about Owen."

"Are you sure?" Lust was clearly riding him hard still because his breathing was still shaky and uneven. She could also see it in his eyes, in the way they darkened when they dropped to her mouth.

Sam licked her lips. "Yes, I'm sure."

Hunter cursed loudly before he took a deep breath and hit Accept. "Hey, what's going on?" he asked as he held the phone to his ear.

On the other line, Hutch's voice sounded panicked. "Hey, sorry to bother you but it's Owen. He's sick. I just took his temperature and I think he's coming down with a cold."

"Oh no," Sam breathed. That meant their night had been cut short. But not surprisingly, she didn't feel too bad about it when she knew he'd be leaving her to go take care of his son.

"Okay, I'm coming." Hunter glanced back at her after he hung up. "I'm sorry," he whispered, "but I—"

Sam held up a hand and nodded. "I know." He didn't have to explain anything to her.

With a look of relief, Hunter stepped forward, gently cupping her face in his hands. Sam smiled up at him, her eyes glittering with happiness.

With his mouth just inches away from hers, the temptation to kiss him again was strong but she stopped herself from indulging. She knew that if she did, they wouldn't be able to stop.

When she tried to pull away, Hunter hung onto her, pulling her back until she was pressed against him. And then, he kissed her with all the desperation and urgency of a man who'd been cut off. Sam laughed when she pulled away. "You're making it damn hard to walk away, Sam," Hunter rasped.

She could only smile sweetly at him in response. "Go," she whispered. "Owen needs you." She needed him too but she could be patient. She could wait. And the next time they were together, it would be even bigger, even more glorious than what'd just happened.

With a rough curse, Hunter yanked his clothes back on. "I'm sorry," he whispered to her when he was by the door.

"It's okay," she said again before he nodded and closed it behind him.

FOURTEEN

WHAT A NIGHT. ALTHOUGH SAM HADN'T GOTTEN what she'd wanted in the end, she couldn't hate Hunter for leaving her when he had. She was well aware of his duties as a father and that would never change simply because he'd started dating her. While this would be a concern for some other women, Sam was independent enough to be fully comfortable with it.

Well, maybe comfortable wasn't the right word. The truth was, she was definitely hot and bothered now that she'd gotten a taste of what a forbidden night with Hunter would be like. Her vibrator that she kept in her bedside table was going to get some action tonight.

But the sudden shrill of her phone ringing had her jumping in her place. Sam hoped it was Hunter calling, but when Deacon's name flashed on the screen, she groaned. "What do you want?" Although she valued her friendship with Deacon, there was only one man she wanted on her mind tonight.

There was a beat before Deacon asked, "What are you doing?"

"I just got home."

"From where?"

"That's none of your business," she snapped.

His tone was knowing. "You were out with someone . . . Who?"

Oh boy. If she didn't just tell him, he'd be bothering her all night. "I was with Hunter."

Deacon made a sound in the back of his throat but Sam decided to ignore it. Instead he asked, "How come you didn't go out with me when I asked you out?"

Her response was automatic. "'Cause you're a manwhore. That's why."

"Ouch. That's cold, Sam." But his tone held no iciness whatsoever. "Whatever. I do have something important to tell you."

"What is it?"

"It's about Clive. He got a lawyer."

"That's not surprising." He had a huge reputation to protect.

"No, that's not the part that worries me. He also claims to have an alibi."

Shit. Really? "Did you check it out?"

"Yes, and get this. It's Brian Melwood."

"You're kidding me." Brian said he'd been at dinner with his wife!

"I wish I was, but Brian confirmed that he did get a call right after Matthew left Clive's house. It's even in the phone records."

"So, what? You think they worked together to try to get rid of Matthew?"

"No. Clive said he had called to try to smooth out the situation between him and Matthew. Brian agreed that it was stupid and wanted to apologize to Matthew too, but then the accident happened and well, you know the rest . . ."

Damn. She did know the rest. And in her visit to Brian after the accident, she didn't suspect any bad blood. Could it really be true? Could they have gotten over their business squabble just like that? Sam wasn't sure about that.

"So now what?" If Clive had an alibi and he was with Matthew for the rest of the night, then how did the brakes on

Matthew's car get damaged?

"I think we have to go back to the suspect pool," Deacon said glumly.

Oh God. What would Hunter think when he heard about all this? Just when she thought the worst was behind them, this happened. Sam hung up and quickly got ready for bed, knowing she had a shit ton of work to do come morning.

As soon as Hunter arrived back home, he made a beeline for Owen's bedroom. "What took you so long?" Hutch asked from his perch beside the bed.

"I got here as quick as I could." It'd been hard to leave Sam like that, but he knew that he really didn't have a choice. He would hate himself later if something happened to Owen.

Hutch rose, giving him room to examine Owen. "I just gave him some medicine." Hunter reached over to touch his son's forehead, taking care not to wake him. He was hot to the touch but he could also see that he was also shivering. Gently, he pulled the covers up higher on him. "Has he had something to eat?" he asked his brother.

"I made him some soup, but he only had half of it."

Hunter threw a surprised look at his brother. "Wait. You made soup?"

"Yeah, I made soup. Don't look at me like that. I know how to cook." While he knew that, he just didn't expect Hutch to go out of his way to do that for him. "So how was your date?" Hutch asked.

Hunter hesitated. Did he really want to know about his brother and best friend's love life? But when Hutch continued to gaze at him expectantly, he sighed. "It was good." Amazing actually. He hadn't wanted it to end.

Hutch threw him a knowing smile. "Sounds like it was

more than a little good. If I recall correctly, you were a little breathless when I called earlier," he teased. "Was I interrupting something?"

Hunter glared at him. *"We are not discussing this!"* He was never one to kiss and tell.

"I don't want the details. But I do want to know if this will make things awkward between us."

"Why would it make things awkward?"

"I just don't want to be caught in the middle if things go to shit."

"Things won't go to shit." Sam had hooked him in like a fish and no amount of jostling or fighting would make him let her go.

"Okay, if you say so." Hutch started for the door but paused. Over his shoulder, he asked, "Are you going to be okay here?"

Hunter glanced down at Owen, sleeping peacefully beside him. "Yeah, we'll be all right." He wasn't going to let anything happen to his little man.

Once he was alone with Owen, Hunter reached over and rubbed his son's cheek. He couldn't believe how quickly he was growing. One day he'd start being interested in girls. What the hell was he going to do with him then?

His thoughts floated to Sam again. Had he been so excited about their date that he'd failed to see the signs of Owen's symptoms before they fully manifested? The guilt started to rise. Maybe if he'd been paying more attention Owen wouldn't have gotten sick.

Beside him, Owen let out a little groan. Hunter reached for him, trying to offer comfort through his touch. Although Hutch had called for him, he'd actually done a really good job of caring for his nephew that all Hunter needed to do now was stay with him.

He eased into the bed beside Owen, careful not to jostle him awake. When he finally found a comfortable position, Owen snuggled up closer to him. His cheeks were flushed pink with his fever and he still looked to be shivering but he'd be all right. They'd both be all right.

In minutes, Hunter was fast asleep, snoring softly beside his son.

FIFTEEN

SAM WOKE UP IN A PISSED-OFF MOOD. AFTER HER frustrating night last night, she went to bed with the hopes to get up early the next morning. But she'd accidentally slept past her alarm and was now being woken up by the annoying sound of her doorbell ringing.

Rolling over, she groaned loudly against her pillow before forcing herself to get out of bed. Whoever this motherfucker was, he or she was going to get it. Why couldn't people ring once, for God's sake! Flinging the door open, Sam came face-to-face with a pimple-faced kid holding a bouquet of flowers. "Are you Ms. Cosi?" he asked her.

"Yes."

"These are for you." The kid pushed the bouquet into her arms and Sam couldn't have looked more confused if she'd tried. *What the hell? Who was sending her flowers?* She checked the card attached to the flowers.

I'm so sorry. I'll make it up to you. Love, H.

"Oh my God." *Hunter had sent her flowers?* "How did he know that peonies are my favorite flowers?" she whispered.

The kid before her took one glance over his shoulder and then stared at her. *Ah right.* How could she be so stupid? Her front garden was full of peonies!

Thanking the kid, Sam took the flowers into her bedroom and set them on her vanity. Leaning in, she gave them a sniff, smiling as the sweet aroma hit her nose. This was a way better wake-up call than her alarm clock.

Once again, she felt kind of silly for making fun of other women who fawned over roses and now look at her, she was becoming one of them! Was this what it was like to fall in love? To have a reason to smile simply because you were thinking about someone else?

She called Hunter immediately, wanting to thank him for his thoughtful gift. But she was entirely unprepared for the rough smoke-and-gravel voice that answered the phone. "Hey, sweetheart. Did you get the flowers?"

"Yes, I got them. Thank you. I love them so much."

"Good. I'm really sorry I had to leave you like that last night. I can assure you, I *really* didn't want to leave." She heard a sound in the background, something soft dragging over skin. Was he still in bed?

She tried to picture what he looked like. His sexy gruff voice was already enough to give her something to build on. Maybe he was shirtless. Or even completely naked in bed, sprawled out like a lazy lion in the sun.

Sam slid beneath her own sheets again, smiling as she did so. "I know you didn't. But don't worry. I'm not mad. How's Owen?"

"He's resting. He woke up a few times in the middle of the night, but I'm hoping he'll be better today."

"Good." She hated to think that he might be suffering.

As a moment of comfortable silence spanned between them, Sam allowed herself to close her eyes and imagine what it would be like to wake up next to Hunter. Even more pleasant was the idea of being able to snuggle up next to Owen too.

"I want to see you again," Hunter whispered.

"You will. But it's probably best that you stay with Owen until he's feeling better." She wondered if Deacon had told him about Clive. She'd been so disappointed that she'd forgotten to ask Deacon about it. But she also didn't want to dim the mood they were in.

"You're right. But do you mind coming by later?"

"Sure." She had some work to do but she desperately wanted to see him again too.

"Good. My dad's coming home today," he said suddenly.

Finally, she thought. *Some good news.* Hopefully having his father back home would lessen the blow that was going to come. Also, it might be her chance to actually ask him some questions. "That's fantastic," she said but she knew she couldn't keep him in the dark any longer. "But there's something I need to tell you."

"What?" She could hear him bracing himself and it saddened her to know that he'd gotten in the habit of hearing bad news for the past few weeks. As she explained what Deacon told her last night, Hunter cursed. "Dammit, I really thought it was all over."

"I'm sorry," she said, truly meaning it. The Happa-Hewitts had gone through so much already.

"It's not your fault. And just so you know, I don't want you looking into this any further. Just leave it up to the police. This is turning out to be a lot more complicated than I anticipated."

"But I can help," she argued. If Deacon needed her, she wouldn't hesitate.

"No," Hunter said firmly. "I don't want you worrying about it. Just leave it alone. Come visit me later. Maybe we can find a moment to be alone . . ."

She'd been so ready to argue with him but the growl in his voice heated her instantly. Dammit. "Fine. I won't do anything. But I still want to see you."

"Good. I'll expect you later then."

"Okay. I can't wait."

Even with a sick kid, Hunter could hardly say he was dreading the day. With the return of his father, he was looking forward to seeing his old man again. And despite what Sam had just told him about Clive, it was a relief to know that he was out of the storm health wise and could finally come home and relax.

When the doorbell rang, Hunter ran for it. He grinned wide as his father came into view, looking way better than the last time he'd seen him. What was even more promising was the fact that he was standing up on his own two feet. Dacey and Hutch still stood on either side of him just in case but Hunter found that he had a lot to be happy about. His family was all together again.

"You gonna keep staring at me like that or are you going to move?" Matthew snapped when he just stood there in place.

He stepped forward. "Here, let me help."

"It's okay," Dacey said. "I've got it."

"Are you sure?"

"Yup. You might want to check outside."

Outside? Glancing over his sister's head, he finally spotted Sam behind her.

"Hey," she said with a shy wave. In her arms she carried a large bag and he belatedly realized it probably contained his father's belongings. "I saw them outside so I figured I'd help out a little bit."

He kissed her before saying, "Let me take those for you. Do you want something to drink?"

"A coffee would be nice."

"Sure thing."

After putting the bags away, he immediately went to make a pot when Sam appeared beside him. "If you're too busy to talk, I can always come back later or something. I know you have a lot going on."

"No, please. Stay." He wouldn't have asked her to come by if he didn't want her around.

"Where's Owen?"

"He's watching TV in his bedroom. I'm happy to announce that he's already on the mend."

"Good. Looks like your father is doing all right too," she said as she tilted her head to the ceiling.

"Yeah. Soon he'll be barking orders and bossing us around again."

Sam laughed at that. God, he loved her laugh. It made his chest tighten in the best way possible. "I want to take you out again. Maybe we can have a redo and start all over."

"Why would I want a redo? Last night was pretty perfect to me."

His smile was quick and so were his reflexes when he reached for her. He probably should be helping his siblings get their father settled but he figured they could manage on their own. Plus, Sam was looking too delicious to ignore. "The ending could've been a little bit better," he drawled.

Sam laughed again. "Yes, it could've been, but I think we can work out an alternate ending."

Suddenly his name was being called and he pulled away. "Want to come up and see my dad?" He knew he'd told her to stay away from the case and let the police handle everything for now, but he couldn't help but think that it would be wasteful to have someone like Sam on their team and not use her. She was too smart to stay on the sidelines.

"Really! But I thought you said ﹘"

"I know. I just worry about you getting hurt or something. But I also know my father would throw a massive fit if he found out that we'd been keeping things from him. I think he's well enough now to take it."

Taking Sam's hand, they both went upstairs together.

Hunter had to admit, Dacey and Hutch had done a good job of getting their father settled in. Matthew was lying comfortably on his big bed, a pile of pillows propping him up. If he didn't know any better, he'd say he looked like a king lying there waiting for his loyal servants to come see him. "Hey, Dad? I know you just got here but Sam would like to ask you some questions . . ."

He motioned for Sam forward and she greeted his father with a small bow. "Hello, Mr. Hewitt."

"Ms. Cosi, how nice to see you."

"I'm glad you're doing better."

"Thank you. It was rough for a bit, but I'm feeling much better now." As he stood on the sidelines, Hunter couldn't help but feel happiness at the strength behind his father's voice. He clearly was recovering well.

"I was wondering if you could help me figure out what happened the night of your accident," Sam said.

As she filled his father in on what had happened, he moved closer to them. "Clive says he was on the phone with Brian trying to sort out the squabble you two had."

"Yeah, that sounds like something he would do." A small smile curled his lips. "He's always trying to smooth out my messes."

"So you're not upset that he's not going to be charged?"

"No," he said to both their surprise. "It's a relief actually. For a moment there, I thought my best friend was trying to kill me."

"But you're the one who told me not to let him take over Gleam," he argued, unable now to keep silent. Why had he done that?

"I did say that, but who am I to question the police? They seem to know what they are doing. I, on the other hand, only remember bits of what happened that night."

Hunter snapped his mouth shut and bit down on his molars. Why wasn't he more upset about this? The father he knew would be in an uproar.

"So there's nothing else you can tell me about who may have done this to you?" Sam asked gently.

Matthew shook his head. "I was with Clive," he said simply. "I'm sorry that I can't help more."

"It's okay."

"Now if you don't mind," Matthew said, "I'd like to take a little nap."

"Sure." Maybe with a little more sleep, he'd be more helpful.

"Thanks for coming to see me, Sam."

Sam grinned down at Matthew. "I promise I'll have this all figured out the next time I see you."

Matthew smiled softly before closing his eyes.

"Let's go back downstairs," Hunter said as they stepped out of the room. "I'm sorry he wasn't more helpful."

"It's okay. It wasn't that bad actually. Besides, he's been through a lot."

Hunter could only nod. His girlfriend was probably more used to this than he was. But it didn't solve the problem still hanging over their heads. Sam brought her hand up to his face. "Hey, don't look so sad. We're going to get through this, okay?"

Hunter nodded and pulled her back into his arms. "Are you planning on staying?" He'd love to spend the day with her.

"No, I should go."

"Aw, come on. Stay for a while."

She poked him playfully in the chest. "You have a job to do and, frankly, so do I."

"You have another case already?"

"No. I just want to check on something."

Hunter pulled back to look at her face. "What are you going to do?"

"I'm going to do what I always do."

"Piss people off?" he teased.

Sam flashed him a brilliant smile. "Actually, that's exactly what I plan to do."

SIXTEEN

S AM HEADED STRAIGHT FOR CLIVE DAVENPORT'S HOME. She knew doing so would probably get her in trouble, but she just couldn't shake the feeling that she'd missed something.

She planned to retrace her steps, to make sure she hadn't accidentally overlooked something that might be pertinent to the case. It wouldn't be the first time she walked by a clue without realizing its significance until later.

When she rang the doorbell, she was surprised to find Clive's son, Mickey, answering the door. He recognized her immediately. "What are you doing here?"

Sam forced herself not to snap back. She knew the reception she'd get by coming here. "Do you mind if I come in?"

"Why? Haven't you people had enough?"

"I just want to ask you a few questions."

Instead of saying no, Mickey tried to slam the door in her face. Sam shot an arm out before it closed on her. "It'll only take a couple of minutes," she insisted. Mickey looked surprised by her strength, which annoyed Sam but she bit back her frustrated growl. "Please," she said softly.

Indecision flashed in his eyes before Mickey finally nodded. He didn't wait for her before walking back into the living room where he sat down and resumed the video game he'd been playing.

Okay, now that she was here, what was she going to say? How was she going to get him to talk? Dammit, she'd come here in such a hurry that she hadn't had time to properly prepare herself. Sam cursed herself before glancing around the room.

Was Clive home? She hoped he wasn't now that she was here. She was likely the last person he'd want to see right now. Slamming a door in her face was tame compared to what she'd done to him.

But Sam couldn't find anything unusual as she looked around so instead she focused her attention back on the video game Mickey was playing. She watched as Mickey "drove" through a series of winding roads. She knew from Hutch that he was playing the latest version of BestDrive, a racing video game that was all the rage apparently.

Mickey seemed to be pretty skilled at the game, maneuvering past several obstacles that stood in his way without a problem. It was only when another car came speeding next to him that Mickey started to lose control. His eyes gleamed with determination as he did his best not to be surpassed by this newcomer. Sam stood there raptured; not by what was happening on the screen though. Her eyes were on Mickey as he played, trying to figure out what she may have missed.

Teeth gritted, Mickey's intensity rose as he leaned forward on the couch. Much like viewers watching the Super Bowl, he was on the edge of his seat, his fingers moving frantically as he did everything he could to beat this guy.

"Son of a bitch!" he barked before slamming the controller down. Sam glanced at the screen. GAME OVER.

Growling, Mickey ran a sweaty hand through his hair and slumped back onto the couch. "So, what do you want?" Although he didn't look in her direction, it amused Sam to see him acting like a wounded puppy. All he'd lost was a round in a stupid video game. But despite being twenty-nine years old, Mickey Davenport still acted like a child.

Sam decided to go with an easy question first. "Is your father here?"

"No."

"Where is he?"

"He's out with that dumb slut."

She felt herself frown. "Dumb slut?"

"Girlfriend," Mickey corrected as he sat back up and pinned his hostile glare on her. "Are you here to try and get some information out of me? So you can try to put all the blame on my father again?" He rose suddenly, crossing the distance between them. "I told you, he didn't do it."

"Then who did?" Sam asked in a calm and level voice. "Because I can assure you that Matthew didn't mess with his own brakes that night."

Mickey's outburst was so sudden that Sam jerked. *"I. Don't. Know!"* he yelled. *"Geez. How many times do I have to tell you that?"*

Worried that he might try to attack her, Sam braced herself, but Mickey simply turned back around and picked the controller back up.

If she was afraid, she didn't show it. She had a feeling that Mickey *did* know something and that was why he was getting so hostile every time she tried to push him. "Matthew Hewitt almost died that night," she continued. "It was lucky he wasn't going any faster or his car would've split right into two by that pole."

"Hallelujah, the man lives." His words dripped with nasty sarcasm. "I really don't care one way or the other." Just like his words suggested, Mickey mentally disengaged from their conversation and focused back on the screen, readying to play another round.

Whatever anger he felt, whatever annoyance, Clive

Davenport's son channeled that aggression into the game. This time Sam focused her attention on the screen. She watched as Mickey dominated the game, his aggression giving him an edge that he hadn't had before. His turns were sharper, his speed faster.

He was good. Real good. Had the first time been a fluke?

Mickey was so preoccupied with the screen before him that he didn't comment when Sam sat down beside him. "Know a lot about cars?" she asked.

"Huh?" He glanced briefly at her then shrugged. "I know enough."

"Do you have your own car?" She hadn't seen one out front, but maybe he kept one in the garage.

"No. I drive my dad's."

His dad's? Sam tried to keep the conversation light but with his focus on winning the game, it seemed that Mickey was more willing to answer her questions. "So how long are you planning on staying with your father?" She knew he'd just come back to Moonrise but she didn't know how long he was going to be here or why he'd returned.

Mickey gave her an impressive side-eye glance. "I don't know yet."

"Can you at least tell me why you came back to Moonrise then?"

This time, Mickey turned to her fully. "So now I need a reason to come visit my dad?" Normally, Sam wouldn't ask that question. But she'd seen him with his father already and knew that they didn't get along. Why would he come visit his father then?

"Where were you the night of the accident?" she asked instead.

"You trying to pin this on me now?"

"Hey," she said, raising her hands up nonthreateningly. "It's just a question."

"My dad is off the hook, okay? And I haven't done shit either." He was yelling now and that was when Sam knew that she had overstayed her welcome. As Mickey paused the game and threw the controller down, she rose.

"Get out!" he growled.

"Fine. I'll leave but you're not helping your own case by doing this."

She made her way to the door to let herself out but paused just long enough to look over her shoulder. Despite his earlier outburst, Mickey had resumed playing his game and when she heard his shout of frustration again, she knew he'd lost. The words GAME OVER flashed on the screen again.

Sam hid her smile.

It certainly was.

SEVENTEEN

AFTER CALLING DEACON AND FILLING HIM IN ON HER latest conversation with Mickey, he told her that he was going to take him in for questioning. "Can you do that?" Sam asked. "Just hold him without concrete evidence?"

"I can do whatever the hell I want." By his tone, it was clear that Deacon was getting frustrated. Despite all his flirting and easy-going personality, the guy took his job very seriously and it seemed that these setbacks were also getting on his nerves. Deacon's voice softened a touch. "We now know that Mickey was in the area when the brakes were tampered with so I'd like a chance to speak to him myself."

Mickey certainly had a strong personality but did his angry, sour character mean that he had tried to kill someone? And what would be his motive? The guy was so well off already. Was he really that greedy that he wanted more?

She didn't realize she'd said it out loud until Deacon said, "That's what I'm going to find out." He hung up without another word.

Damn. Well, at least now the police were taking this more seriously. Hopefully they'd get it all sorted sooner rather than later.

Sam had just walked through her front door when her cell phone rang. "Hey, Hunter," she said as she answered.

"Sam, can you do me a big favor?" His voice sounded rushed and a little panicked.

"Sure. What is it? Is something wrong?"

"The meeting that I'm in is running long, but Owen's babysitter called and said that she needs to leave soon for a concert. Do you think you can pick him up for me?"

"Absolutely. No problem." *Pick up a kid. How hard could it be*? Plus, she'd missed getting a chance to spend some quality time with Owen. She was looking forward to it.

"Thank you," Hunter breathed. "You're a life saver." He quickly rattled off the babysitter's address.

Within ten minutes Sam was walking up to the doorstep, ringing the babysitter's doorbell. A young teenager wearing a band T-shirt and ripped jeans opened the door. Sam had to admit, she looked to have some good taste in fashion. With shoulder-length blonde hair, the tips dyed a bright pink color. In one ear, she also had multiple piercings that glinted when the sun hit it.

"Can I help you?" she asked when Sam just stood there, staring at her.

Sam smiled. "Hi, you must be Cybil. I'm here to pick up Owen."

In response, the teenager started to close the door on her. Sam reacted quickly, reaching out to stop it from banging into her nose. "Hey! What the hell!" Unlike Mickey, this girl had no reason to slam the door in her face!

"You're not taking Owen!" the babysitter squawked.

"Jesus, are you crazy? I'm his babysitter!"

"No, *I'm* the babysitter," the girl shot back.

"Okay," Sam allowed. They both needed to cool it before her neighbors came out to see what the ruckus was about. "What I mean to say is, I'm here to take Owen to his father. He's caught up in a meeting." Sam had no idea what she'd done to cause this reaction from Owen's babysitter, but she was really questioning Hunter's decision on hiring this girl. She may look cute, but she was clearly a psycho.

She'd just managed to wrestle the door open when Owen appeared behind Cybil. "There you are!" she called out. "Get your stuff! We're leaving!"

Owen gawked at her. She bet they looked ridiculous fighting for dominance at the door. "What are you guys doing?" the kid asked.

As soon as the other girl heard his voice, she froze. "Wait. You know her?"

Owen nodded. "She's my dad's—"

"Girlfriend," Sam supplied.

"*Girlfriend,*" the other girl squawked. "I didn't know Mr. Happa-Hewitt was seeing someone!"

"He is. He's dating *me.* That's why I'm here. He called me and asked me to pick Owen up."

Cybil shot a wary look at Owen. "How come he never told me you were coming?"

He hadn't? Crap. No wonder why she'd been acting so strangely! But he probably didn't have the time before he had to return to his meeting. Cybil probably thought she was some psycho trying to kidnap Owen. "You know what? Let me just call him again so you can speak to him. I'm sure that will clear everything up." She told Owen to grab his things while she made the call.

"So, you're saying . . . he's not single anymore?" Sam craned her head back to the babysitter. *Oh no,* she thought as soon as she saw Cybil's face. She knew that look. It seemed that she wasn't the only one here who had a thing for Mr. Happa-Hewitt. Did Hunter know that his babysitter had a massive crush on him? She made a mental note to question him later. "How long?" the girl demanded.

"Uh, I don't know." Things hadn't really occurred in the

way a normal relationship would've between them. She wasn't even sure when it all began. Had it started when Hunter had come to her office, asking for her help? Or had it begun when he'd asked her out on their first official date? "How old are you anyway?" she asked instead.

"I'm twenty." Hmm. Hunter was thirty-three. "I think he's a bit old for you, hon."

Cybil sounded dejected. "Yeah. I guess."

Despite how quickly things had gone south when they'd first met, Sam actually liked this girl. "So what concert are you going to?" she asked.

The babysitter immediately perked up. "I'm going to see Sebastian McQueen." She said his name like he was a god.

Sam shook her head. "Never heard of him." To be honest though, she hardly paid attention to what was trending. She'd always been still stuck in her own little world.

Cybil gasped. "How can you even say that?" Sam simply shrugged in answer. "You're probably too old."

Sam laughed. "Touché." It seemed that all the tension from earlier had dissipated. That was when Owen returned with his school backpack hauled over one shoulder. Sam immediately took it from him and guided him out. "Bye, Cybil," Owen called out when he was halfway to the car.

Sam turned back and waved goodbye too. "Have fun tonight," she said.

"Thanks," Cybil called out. "Will I see you again?"

She was going to answer with an, "I don't know" since this had just been a favor for Hunter, but if she planned on being with him for the long run, it was likely she'd be seeing more of her. "Yes. Definitely."

Cybil shot her a smile and Sam couldn't help but think what a nice girl she was as she pulled out of the driveway.

The summer sun had long set when Hunter got out of the office and now he was dying to see his son. After making sure that Maison got home safely, Hunter headed straight for Sam's place. Hopefully she hadn't received too much grief from Cybil when she'd gone to pick Owen up. The teen tended to be a little protective of his kid but that was what he liked about her. Cybil always went above and beyond what he expected someone her age would do for a job; that was why he'd hired her in the first place.

He remembered how stressed he'd been when the divorce had just happened and he had to find a new babysitter for Owen. Both Dacey and his father had given him suggestions but none of them had been good enough.

At first, he'd never understood his father's protectiveness of his kids, mostly because it'd been such a pain in the ass growing up. But now that he had his own kid to care for, Hunter knew just how stressful it was to find someone you trusted to care for your child.

That was why he'd called Sam when he knew he couldn't make it. He could trust her with anything. It also helped that Owen had a particular fondness for his girlfriend.

He knocked softly on the door, not wanting to wake Owen up if he was already sleeping. But when Sam opened the door, he was surprised to see Owen wide-eyed and awake, watching cartoons on her couch. "Hey," he said before dropping a kiss to Sam's lips.

"Hey yourself. What took you so long?"

"Sorry. Things are super busy right now." And now he was exhausted.

Taking his hand, Sam settled back into her spot next to Owen. "Come sit down." She patted the seat beside her, and Hunter dove right in, happy to feel her next to him. He let out a long groan as he stretched out his tired legs. Despite sitting in a chair all day, he was aching in places he never had before.

"Do you want some dinner?" Sam asked him. "There's still some spaghetti."

"In a bit." He wanted to rest for a while. Hunter closed his eyes, happy to finally be able to relax. Within seconds, he was already dozing off.

"Daddy?"

Hunter forced himself to open his eyes and look at his kid. "What's up?" He reached out and ruffled his small head.

"Can I have a girlfriend?"

"Huh? Wh—what?" The question caught him so off guard that he sat up in a jolt. "Why do you want a girlfriend?" He'd figured this time would come, but he never expected it to come *this* early.

"'Cause you have one."

Hunter glanced at Sam and she promptly burst into laughter. "What are you laughing about?"

Sam cupped her face in her hands. "You should see your expression right now. It's hilarious."

He was tired and his brain wasn't working properly. "Do you know what he's going on about?"

"Cybil," she explained. "She likes you. Did you know that?"

"No, she doesn't." He would've known if that was the case.

"She does. She looked like she was going to maul me when I told her we were dating."

"You told her we were dating?"

"Yeah." Sam suddenly looked wary. "Was that wrong of me to do?"

"God, no."

"Good," Sam said with a smile. It still thrilled him every time she looked at him like that.

"But did she say that she liked me or—" Sam slapped him in the chest. *"Ow!"*

"She's too young for you!"

Now it was his turn to laugh at her expression. "You're right. Besides," he said, leaning further into her, "I already have the girl I want." After dropping a kiss on her mouth, he turned back to Owen. "You can have a girlfriend but I think you'll want to wait a little bit."

"Why?"

"You've got some growing up to do."

"So I can have a girlfriend when I'm bigger?"

"Absolutely." Although he was already dreading the day when that happened. It would mean that his little guy was all grown up. "So have you been having fun with Sam?"

Owen nodded and Sam laughed. "Good." He ruffled his hair again. "I'm glad."

As Owen turned back to watch his cartoons, Sam rose and moved to the kitchen. When she returned, she handed him a bowl of spaghetti. "Come on, take it," she said when he just stared at her. "It'll get cold again."

"You're too good to me. I could've gotten it myself, you know." Except it seemed that his bones had melted as soon as he'd sat down on the couch. It was that comfy. Sam returned to her spot next to him as he picked up the fork. "Thank you," he whispered before he took his first bite.

"No problem."

Sam's phone rang suddenly and she got up to answer it. "Oh no," she said when she saw the name on the screen. "It's my mom."

"Answer it."

"Fine." But she didn't sound too happy about it. "Hey, Mom," she said into the phone. "Yes, I'm very excited about the

wedding tomorrow." She paused and then said, "Of course my dress is ready."

Although he'd been focused on his food just a second ago, Hunter was now far more interested in Sam's conversation. He listened intently as he ate.

Sam now spoke in hushed tones, acting like she didn't want him to overhear her but he was still catching bits and pieces here and there. "Yes, yes, I will. Don't worry, okay, Mom. It'll all work out."

She hung up shortly after that but the tension didn't ease from her body. "Is everything okay?" he asked.

Sam turned back toward him, her expression morphing into something he'd never seen before. Wait a minute. Was Sam *embarrassed?*

"Uh, Hunter?" she started. "There's something I need to ask you . . ."

"What is it?"

"Do you want to go to my sister's wedding with me tomorrow?" Hunter couldn't hide his shock. "I know it's a lot to ask and I haven't really given you much notice but—"

Was Sam Cosi actually asking him to be *her date?* Normally this wouldn't be such a trial for other couples, but he knew to Sam that this was a big deal.

He didn't hesitate. "Of course."

"Really? You'll come? I mean, I don't want to force you and you don't have to just because—" Her face was getting red and he found it adorably cute.

"Sam, Sam, it's all right. I *do* want to go." He was just really happy that she'd asked him. He took her hand in his, trying to reassure her.

"Okay," she said with a smile, seeming relieved. "I'm really glad."

"So does this mean I'll get to meet the rest of your family?"

Her pinched expression told him that she wasn't too thrilled with the idea. "Not that I don't want you to meet them or anything it's just . . ."

"They're a lot to handle?"

"Yes," she breathed.

Now it was his turn to smile. "Do you remember who you're talking to?"

Sam laughed. "Well, my family is different. They're a little more . . . vocal about things."

"They tell it to you straight?" Is that why Sam was so direct all the time?

"Yes. Especially my mother."

"I'm looking forward to it."

Sam looked at him like he'd just admitted he was looking forward to torture. "Are you sure?"

He pulled her into his arms. "Yes, I'm sure."

"Okay, but don't say I didn't try to warn you."

Hunter pulled her in closer. "It'll be fine. In fact, I think it might actually be fun."

EIGHTEEN

HUNTER HAD WORN HIS BEST SUIT. WHILE HE'D gotten used to dressing up for work now, he still hadn't put that much effort into it. Today, however, he wanted to look extra polished for the wedding. He honestly didn't care about the bride or groom. What did concern him was Sam. He wanted to make a good impression for her because he knew how nervous she was going to be.

While Sam wasn't the type to care about what other people thought about her, he couldn't stand the thought that there would be people out there who would be looking down on her just because she hadn't brought a date with her. Now that he was her boyfriend, he had no intention of ever having Sam stand alone against her meddling mother.

Now at the church as Serena and Aaron had said their vows, his gaze kept returning to Sam. She'd completely shocked him—and probably a lot of her other family members—by the beautiful dress she'd worn. He was so used to seeing her in jeans and a leather jacket that seeing her in a pale pink dress had completely devastated him. If he thought her beautiful then, she was angelic now.

With hair falling in soft waves around her face, Sam wore minimal makeup. Since her dress was strapless, her chest and back were on full display. The large tattoo of angel wings spanning her shoulders reminded him of her rebellious streak, and Hunter smiled. He liked Sam's rough edges. It was what made her unique, and paired with her frilly dress, she made quite the

sight. He was glad he'd come with her today because he probably wouldn't be the only one admiring her tonight.

During the entire ceremony, she'd kept turning back to
look at him. Probably just to make sure that he hadn't bolted already. But he honestly couldn't see what she was worried about.
Sure, her mother was a little more vocal about her thoughts but
he kind of liked that about her. It showed her strong will and it
also reminded him of another woman he knew.

So when the shouting first started, Hunter simply assumed
that it was Rosanna at it again. He didn't realize it wasn't her
until a woman launched herself up on the altar. *"What the hell?"*

Everyone around him gasped.

"You're going to regret this!" the woman screamed. Spittle
flew from her mouth as a man grabbed hold of her and tried to
pull her back.

"I can't believe she'd come here!" someone behind him
said.

What? Who was this woman?

The bride looked like she was going to say something, but
Sam pulled her sister back. "I'll handle this," she said as she
stomped toward the other woman. Hunter was by her side in
an instant, ready to protect her by any means necessary. "What
the hell are you doing here, Alyssa?" Sam snapped. "You know
you're not supposed to be here."

"Can someone *please* kick her out?" Rosanna asked from
behind him.

Hunter's eyes went wide before he leaned in. "Want to tell
me who this crazy woman is?"

"She's Aaron's ex-girlfriend," Rosanna answered. "She's
been trying to stop this wedding from happening ever since he
and Serena started dating."

Alyssa gave a shout as she fought against another man who

was trying to pull her away. *Jesus. Was this what Sam meant about craziness?*

Sam took a menacing step forward. Despite wearing a pink, flowy dress, her stance projected authority and everyone in the church stopped to look at her. "Let go of her!" she shouted. The two men immediately released Alyssa.

Then, Sam surged forward and grabbed a hold of the woman's arms. "Let's go."

"No, I'm—" She tried to pull free.

"Let's go, Alyssa." Both Sam's tone and gaze demanded obedience and after a moment, the woman relented. "Keep going!" Sam ordered over her shoulder as she led the woman away.

But Hunter had no plans to stay to watch the wedding. He ran after Sam. "Should I be calling the cops?" He had no idea how to handle this!

Sam pushed Alyssa into a small room, forcing her to sit on a chair. "Stay there," she ordered. "And if you try to run, so help me God I will—"

Sam looked like she wanted to commit murder with the way her eyes were boring into the other woman. Hunter pulled out his phone and called Deacon just to be safe. He didn't know this woman but knew she was definitely unstable.

He still had the phone up to his ear when Sam turned and approached him. "I'm going to stay here and make sure she doesn't interrupt things a second time."

"I'm calling Deacon right now," he told her. While he was definitely overqualified for this, his buddy was always more than willing to help him out when he was in a bind. "Don't worry, she won't be able to do it again."

Sam nodded. But it appeared that Alyssa had heard it too because her head snapped in their direction and she bolted from her chair.

Hunter's eyes went wide with panic. *"Sam, watch out!"*

Sam swung around, surprised to find Alyssa on her feet and making a beeline for her. "Son of a bitch!" Before she could reach her, Sam pushed her to the ground until she was practically on top of her. Alyssa screamed and bucked, but Sam held firm, doing her best to keep her immobile.

Hunter was beside her in the next instant. "Holy shit. Are you okay?"

"I'm fine," she gritted. It was Alyssa who he should be worried about. She'd likely press charges on her for tackling her to the ground like that. Luckily, Hunter had informed her that Deacon was on his way. She only hoped that the wedding wouldn't be ruined when the cops arrived.

"That was pretty amazing," Hunter mused. Now that she was sure Alyssa wouldn't be causing more trouble for them, Sam allowed herself to return the smile. She was so happy that he'd agreed on coming with her today. He'd saved her from having to endure the scrutiny from her family. And her mother seemed to be absolutely head over heels in love with Hunter already.

"You're the best, you know that?" she said before kissing him.

When he pulled back, his dark eyes blazed with desire. "I think you're the one who just proved you're the best."

"Hey!" Alyssa snapped from below her. "I'm still here!"

"And that's where you'll stay until the cops arrive," she snarled. Hopefully once this was all over, she'd stop bothering her sister.

When cops finally arrived, Sam was surprised that Deacon wasn't with them. He was likely trying to figure out the Happa-Hewitt case still but the officer in his place was more than capable of handling things. After she quickly debriefed them on what happened, he took Alyssa away, reassuring her that he'd handle the rest. Sam had never felt so relieved. She felt terrible for letting things get this far.

Although she'd missed most of the actual wedding, things actually hadn't gotten too bad. At least her sister was finally married now. Upon seeing her, Serena made a beeline for her. "Sam, I can't believe what you did in there! You single-handedly saved the wedding!"

Sam raised her hands up. "Okay, I wouldn't go as far and saying that but—"

Her younger sister embraced her hard. "You did! Thank you!" The people around her cheered and Sam felt herself start to blush.

"Okay, okay. That's enough," she said, pushing Serena off her. "I'm just glad the wedding went through." As much as she hated weddings, she knew this day was important for her sister.

"You're the best sister ever!"

"And you make a beautiful bride."

Aaron appeared beside them and shot her a smile. "Thank you, Sam. What you did back there was pretty badass."

"You're welcome."

She watched as Serena embraced Aaron and he leaned down to kiss her. It was a kiss of newlywed bliss and, therefore, it went on longer than she thought appropriate in front of a lot of people. *Eww.*

Excusing herself, Sam finally turned back to Hunter.

His dark eyes were wild as he watched her walk over to him. If only they could ditch this place and go home but they still had the reception to go to. "So do you see why I like to live alone? Nothing ordinary happens with my family."

A dark grin made an appearance before he nodded. "You're

certainly right about that. I have never, *ever* seen that happen at a wedding before."

Sam laughed. "Trust my family to be the first to do it."

"Don't worry, it's over now." Hunter reached out and grabbed a hold of her hand. "Come on. Let's get out of here."

"Wait. Where are we going? We can't leave now!"

"Shh, it'll only be a few minutes." Hunter just wanted to hold her in his arms. But he knew that with so much of her family around, she wouldn't want to make a scene so he was going to take her some place more private.

To be honest, he'd been scared as shit when Alyssa had tried to attack her. The only other time he'd felt that kind of heart-stopping moment was with Owen or recently with his father and the accident. But seeing that woman making a beeline for Sam made his heart race with fear.

And that was how he knew Sam Cosi had become someone more to him than he ever expected.

Although he knew she was more than capable of handling herself, he was still surprised with how quickly she'd managed to take Alyssa down. There was no question about it now. Sam Cosi was a total badass.

From the very first moment they'd met, he'd always found her intriguing. He probably could've been friendlier to her in the beginning, but that was only because he wasn't used to women who were as independent or as outspoken as she was.

Never in a million years would he have thought they would be compatible, but now, Hunter was seeing Sam for what she truly was—a sexy, intelligent woman who could definitely give him a run for his money.

He realized he liked her. *A lot.* And he was really hoping that he could continue seeing her. He already knew that Owen liked her. Hell, Hutch did as well. He'd seen no reason for the rest of the family to not get on board with her.

But would it be too soon? After his ex-wife's betrayal, he'd never thought he could fall this quickly with someone else. But he had. Sam was just too amazing for words.

Hunter caught himself. He had no idea why he was suddenly thinking about all this. Maybe it was the fact that they were at a wedding, but things were still brand new between him and Sam. He was excited to see where they would go.

"Are we just going to keep walking?" Sam asked as they strolled through the beautiful paths near the church. "I mean, it's beautiful and all, but they'll probably be looking to take photos of me soon." But then that mischievous smile he adored so much made an appearance. "Are you trying to lure me away to seduce me?"

"Maybe I am," he whispered, drawing his lips closer to hers. "What are you going to do about it?"

"I'll tackle you to the ground like I did with Alyssa."

His eyes flashed with heat. "I'd like that."

Sam's laughter only made him smile even more. He was just about to kiss her when the officer from earlier cleared his throat. They pulled apart reluctantly.

"Ah, sorry to interrupt but Detective Thorpe would like to speak to you two." He held out a cell phone and Sam reached out for it.

"Hello?"

Deacon's voice was loud and clear on the speakerphone. "Hey, Sam. Is Hunter there with you?"

"I'm right here." He wondered why Deacon hadn't shown up after he'd spoken to him earlier . . .

"Hey, sorry about earlier. But something else held me up. Anyway, I just wanted to tell you that we got him."

Wait. "What?"

"We found some files earlier in Mickey's bedroom about Matthew. Sam, you were right." Beside him, Sam breathed out harshly. "The guy's got motive. Apparently he *hates* Matthew Hewitt."

Mickey? So it'd been Mickey? "So you mean—" He felt his chest tighten.

"Yes. It looks like Mickey was the one who tampered with the brakes. Not Clive. We didn't know he was even around that night so we never questioned him."

Hunter felt like someone had just punched him in the gut. "Holy shit," he breathed.

"I know," Deacon said. "It's a lot to take in but I think it's over now."

Over? Thank God.

He couldn't believe how tangled this entire thing had gotten. He had to give the Moonrise Beach Police Department a lot of credit. Most of the evidence had been washed away in the rain that night and since Matthew had been in recovery, they couldn't go to him and ask him what they wanted. They could only go on what they already knew and whatever small clues they'd found.

"How do you feel?" Sam asked as she reached out to comfort him.

Sam.

Sam had helped Deacon again? Even after he asked her not to? Well, he guessed he couldn't be mad at her. This was what she did, what she was good at. It was cruel of him to ask her to leave it alone.

"I'm fine. I guess. I just need to get behind the idea that Mickey would do this." He didn't particularly like the guy. In fact, he *hated* him, but he didn't realize that the guy harbored that much hatred for his family that he'd try to get one of them killed.

Sam nodded. "It's all been a little crazy, hasn't it?"

"Yeah." He turned toward her again, pulling her back into his arms. "But it's okay." He didn't want to think about Gleam or the case right now. He'd deal with that later. He just wanted to be here for Sam.

"Now, where were we?" he murmured as he dropped his head toward her.

Sam's smile was brilliant as she looked up at him. "I believe you were going to kiss me."

"Oh, yes." His mouth hovered just inches from hers. Closing his eyes, he allowed everything around them to disappear.

A frustrated growl erupted from Sam's throat before she grabbed the back of his neck and kissed him hard. Hunter poured everything into that kiss, letting go of all thought and sensation.

"There you are!" a voice called out. "Stop sucking face and get over here! We've got photos to take!"

Dammit.

They separated once again, both of them panting hard. Sam shot an irritated growl at her sister but didn't say anything as she took his hand. "Let's go back before they come over here."

Hunter smiled and followed her back to her family.

NINETEEN

IT WAS NO SURPRISE THAT MICHAEL DAVENPORT'S ARREST made the headlines. For days the media loitered outside Gleam Enterprises, trying to get a glimpse of Clive as he came in to work.

Since they'd wrongly accused Clive of being responsible for the accident, they'd apologized and allowed him back to the office. Things were still a little strained whenever they crossed paths but it looked like Clive was happy to return. Hunter hadn't brought up Mickey to him though, so he wasn't sure how he felt about that, but he and the police were still determined to find out what happened that night.

Thankfully, his father was already out of the hospital and would be returning to reclaim his position soon. Hunter just wasn't sure how the relationship between Clive and his father would be after this. Hopefully, the company wouldn't suffer more than it already had.

By the end of the day, Hunter was desperate to get home and see his family. Before heading for his car, he pulled out his cell phone and called Sam. She picked up on the third ring. "Hello?"

"Hey, baby. How was your day?"

"Good."

"Where are you?"

"I just got home actually. I'm about to jump in the shower."

"Can I join you?"

His grin widened as Sam laughed. "Sure, but I don't see

how that's possible with you being there and I'm here."

Damn, she had a point. "I'll be leaving here in a few minutes to pick up Owen."

"Do you want me to pick him up?" Sam offered.

"No, it's fine. You've had a long day. But I'd love it if you came over for dinner later."

"Sorry but I can't. I'm having dinner with my neighbor tonight."

Disappointment bloomed in his chest. "No worries then."

"Can I stop by after?"

"Really?"

"Yeah."

"Then I'll see you later."

"Be ready to open the door so I don't have to ring the doorbell and risk waking everyone up."

"Don't worry." He was going to be ready.

Sam hated herself. She really, *really* hated herself. She never thought she was the kind of woman who pined for a man like this, but here she was, counting down the minutes until she got to see Hunter. It seemed that the more time she spent with him, the more she wanted him.

Although she initially dreaded going to her sister's wedding, Sam actually discovered that she enjoyed herself. Not only were people surprised by her bringing a date, but they all seemed to really like Hunter, her mother especially.

Rosanna had gone on and on about Hunter, which was funny since she'd only met him a few hours prior to the wedding, but Sam was just glad that her mother had finally stopped pushing men onto her and was actually happy for her for once. She really needed to figure out how to say thank-you to him.

She'd started a new case today, one not involving cars and

billionaires. But she still found it fairly interesting. That was one of the things she loved about her job. No two cases were alike.

Sam was also looking forward to her dinner with Amara tonight. With her busy work schedule, they hadn't been able to keep up with their weekly dinners. Sam made sure to make some time this week. It'd been too long and she missed chatting with her friend.

Later that evening, they talked about Amara's family life and her dating life. Sam found herself relaxing more and more. With the Happa-Hewitt case and the wedding behind her, she could finally relax and enjoy pleasant company. They talked about gardening, another one of Sam's favorite topics, and by the end of the night, Sam was sad to see Amara leave.

They'd had such a great time that she didn't realize how late it was already and a pang of guilt went through her. She hoped Hunter wouldn't be mad at her. She texted him quickly, hoping that he was still awake.

His answering text was immediate. *I miss you.*

Sam smiled at the three simple words. "I miss you too," she said aloud. She never thought she could miss someone when she'd just seen him, but she couldn't wait to see him again. After quickly texting him to tell him that she was coming over, Sam jumped into her car and drove the short distance from her house to the Happa-Hewitts'.

Giddiness shot through her as she walked to the front door. She was thankful when the doors opened immediately and Hunter stood there, wearing a mischievous smile and a tight-fitting T-shirt that showed off all his sexy muscles. "Hello, handsome." She didn't hesitate as she closed the distance between them and kissed him hotly on the lips, pouring every bit of her need into it. Hunter pulled her even closer, pressing her back into the door and the hard wall of his body. When he pulled back, the both of them were panting.

"Let's go inside."

Sam looked around and noticed that most of the lights were off. "Where is everyone?" And then she remembered how late it was. "Oh crap. Maybe I shouldn't have come." Not like they could do much while everyone else was asleep.

"It's fine. Let's sit for a little bit." Taking her hand, he led them to the large leather couch in the living room.

"Hey!" she squeaked as he pulled her down onto him.

"Shh."

"Sorry!"

Dropping her mouth to his again, she kissed him with a tenderness that was unlike her. Usually she liked things fast and hard, but with Hunter, she wanted to savor the moment.

Hunter broke the kiss first and groaned. "Dammit, Sam, you're making this really hard for me."

Hard? "How hard?" she asked with a dangerous glint in her eyes.

"Sam," he warned. "Don't."

"Why not?" Her hand was already lowering to his hips. But Hunter flipped them over until *she* was the one on her back.

"Oh!" How did he move so quickly? How could she complain though? In this position, she had all six feet two of sexy Happa-Hewitt muscle on her.

God, this was a bad idea. A *very* bad idea. Hunter's magic hands started to work on her as he continued to kiss her with growing need. Sam felt like a cat in heat, rubbing up against him as sensation buffeted her body.

With a grunt, Hunter pushed her back into the cushions before pulling her bra down so that her breasts spilled free.

Then his mouth was on them, teasing and tasting, plucking them with his fingers. "Oh!" Sam gasped. "That feels so good."

In the darkness, Hunter's eyes met hers, glowing with intensity and need. Through the thrumming of blood in her ears, she could hear him panting heavily, could feel the way his chest rose and fell. She reached out, intending to touch his face when Hunter dipped his head and blew a hot stream of air over her nipple.

"Oh my God!"

It was pleasure and torture mixed in one, and by the time he took them into his mouth again, Sam was a whimpering mess. She could feel herself growing wet for him. And her nipples tightened with every glorious stroke of his tongue.

"*Hunter*," she gasped as his hand had found the hot place between her thighs. He ground his palm against her core, creating friction where she needed it the most. "Yes, more."

"You're so fucking hot," Hunter moaned before he took a nipple into his mouth again. Teeth scraped until a squeak escaped her lips. *Oh shit! She hoped nobody heard that!*

Hunter certainly did because he had this amused, devilish smile on his face that wasn't helping her situation at the moment. He resembled a big, hungry wolf who was going to eat her alive. As his hand continued to do magical things to her body, Sam allowed herself to feel.

She'd been so desperate for him that she didn't care what the time was or where they were. She wanted this moment, to feel him against her, knowing that she didn't have to let go.

She wasn't even aware of the sounds she was making until a large hand clamped over her mouth and her eyes snapped open again. "You have to be quiet, sweetheart. You'll wake everyone up."

Sam was too far gone to comply. Her blood was roaring in

her ears and she was pretty sure her bones had melted because she couldn't move.

How foolish she'd been to think this wouldn't happen. They were acting like a pair of teenagers, trying to get as far as they could without getting caught.

It made Sam smile. She never thought she'd be in this position again. Her whole life had been about trying to prove herself. To show that she was stronger, smarter, better than what others thought her to be. But Sam never felt like she had to prove anything when she was with Hunter. He seemed to like her exactly how she was.

Her breath caught as her orgasm grew nearer. She would've been embarrassed except for the fact that Hunter seemed to be getting off on watching her like this. The pressure built until she was clutching at him and the cushions.

When she came, she came intensely. Her teeth bit into one fist to attempt to muffle the cry that tore from her throat. Her pussy clamped down on emptiness and she suddenly wished Hunter had filled her instead of making her come against his hand.

Still, she was more than satisfied by the smoking-hot orgasm he'd just given her. He'd certainly made up for him leaving her the other night.

"Damn, that was hot." Hunter's voice was shot even though it seemed like she'd been the one who'd done all the screaming. "You're so sexy when you come."

A wash of color flooded her face. "Do you think anyone heard that?"

"I fucking hope not because I'm sporting an erection as big as the Eiffel Tower right now."

That got a burst of laughter from her. She clamped her hand over her mouth. "Well, I have a way of fixing that."

Hunter groaned as she reached for him. "You're killing me."

Sam slid off the couch and dropped to her knees, pressing Hunter back into the couch so that he lay relaxed. She couldn't believe how easy she'd unraveled for him, but now she hoped to return the favor.

"Sam, we can't—"

She batted his hand away. "You started this." When she reached for him again, Hunter didn't stop her. Slowly, she eased his zipper down, flicking her gaze back up to him as moans slipped past his lips. She wasn't surprised to find that his cock was proportionate to the rest of his body.

For a moment, Sam just took her time getting to know him. Her fingers couldn't quite meet around him, and she quite liked the fact that he veered slightly to the left when fully aroused. The big mushroom tip made her mouth water and the thick vein running down the length made her want to get down on her knees and worship him.

Sam jacked him off slowly at first, and then added another hand when he started to breathe more heavily. When the tip of her tongue darted out to taste him, his hips jackknifed off the couch.

"Sam," he breathed.

Sam smiled. Even in the moonlight, she could see his eyes rolling back in pleasure when she took him all the way to the back of her throat.

She did that a few more times, liking how his hips started to move. She loved seeing him this way, on the verge of losing control. She got the feeling that Hunter didn't let his guard down very often so the fact that she was with him made her very happy.

Hunter suddenly lurched forward and grabbed a fistful of

her hair. Before she could fully register that, his hips snapped forward and he held her there. Sam was forced to breathe through her nose and once he released her, she gasped. *Oh my God.* Hunter let out a string of expletives. "Holy fuck, Sam." His breathing was ragged and uneven, and a fine sheen of sweat covered his entire body. "You're killing me here. There's no way I can be silent when I come."

"That's fine with me." Hell, she'd be fine with whatever he wanted.

"No," he rasped. "I don't want to hold back when I'm with you."

"Then don't." She licked a wet line up his length and Hunter bit out another curse. She'd never been so turned on giving a man a blowjob; she was sure her panties were soaked by now.

She knew the moment when he lost it. Hunter's entire body stiffened before a guttural roar ripped from his throat. Hot streams of semen shot out onto her hand as she stroked him through his orgasm.

Finally, when he relaxed, Sam brought her hand to her mouth and licked her fingers. Hunter immediately pushed himself up from the couch and took her face in his hands. "Do you think anyone heard that?" she whispered.

"Maybe." A sinful smirk curled his lips. "I wasn't exactly quiet when I came." No, he'd practically roared at the ceiling. "But that's all on you," he added.

"*Me?*"

"You should've warned me."

"You should have better control," she shot back.

"Honey, I have no control when it comes to you." Satiated and content, they both stretched out on the couch, simply listening to the sounds of each other's heartbeats.

That had been by far the most desperate, hungry sex she'd

ever had. Never in her life had she felt so needy like that. But she guessed that was to be expected when she hadn't seen him since the wedding and they hadn't been able to slake their lust since their first date.

When she reached for him again, Hunter dropped his hand over her mouth. "Wait. Are you going to be noisy again?"

She felt herself smile. "Depends on what you're going to do to me."

"You don't want to know, Sam," he said as he lowered himself to her once again. "You don't want to know."

TWENTY

MORNING LIGHT SHONE THROUGH THE WINDOWS as Hunter woke. Glancing over, he smiled at the sight beside him. Sam was there, snoozing, her full lips parted ever so slightly as she snored. He'd always wondered what it would be like waking up next to her and he found the experience more pleasurable than he could've ever imagined.

Reaching out, he brushed his fingertip across her forehead, pushing a stray strand of hair away from her face. Sam stirred, moaning as she stretched before slowly opening her eyes. "Good morning," he said as he grinned down at her.

Sam winced as the sunlight hit her eyes. "Ugh, what time is it?"

"I don't know. But it's early."

"I'd better go." Sam moved to sit up but Hunter stopped her.

"Don't you want to stay for breakfast?" He wasn't ready for her to leave yet.

"You don't think it'll be weird?"

"Why would it be weird?"

"I don't know. What if Owen asks what I'm doing here so early?"

"I doubt he'll mind."

For a second, it looked like Sam wanted to argue but then she smiled. "Fine, I'll stay." Although Sam was more forward than most women, there were times where she felt shy and this was one of those rare moments.

"Good." Sitting up, he kissed her before heading for the kitchen. "Do you want to shower or something?"

"No, I'll do that when I get home." As he started making coffee for them, Sam tidied up the living room.

When she finally joined him in the kitchen, he pulled her into his arms. "I've got to wake up Owen and get him ready for school."

"Do you want me to make breakfast then?"

"Nah, I can do it."

"But I'm already here. What do you want to eat? Eggs? French toast?"

"Okay. Any one of those would be great."

"I'll make French toast," she decided.

"Thanks." He headed for the stairs as she started pulling ingredients from the fridge. He made a beeline for Owen's room, not surprised at all to find his pillows scattered on the ground. What was with this kid? Every morning his stuff was always on the ground. Hunter bent to pick everything up and said, "Time to wake up, buddy. We've got to get you to school."

A little groan sounded from beneath the covers and a smile broke out over his face. Poor kid. Much like him, he wasn't a morning person but he'd had to become one recently. The only proven way to get Owen out of bed was to tickle him.

So that's what Hunter did. He started small, going for the sensitive part behind Owen's ear. When his son began to stir, he moved lower to his neck. Giggles started to tumble out of Owen's mouth but Hunter didn't stop there. When he reached for the kid's most ticklish part, right beneath his arm, full-on guffaws flowed out.

"All right, that's enough." He pulled back when he saw Owen was gasping between his laughter. "We've got to get moving." They didn't want to be late again. "By the way," Hunter said, knowing what he said next would really get the kid moving. "Sam is downstairs making breakfast for us."

"Sam is here?"

"Yup."

"Yay! I love Sam!"

He did too. They showered and dressed quickly and by the time they returned downstairs, he was surprised to find that Sam wasn't alone anymore. His father was out of bed and sitting at the table with her, eating his own plate of French toast. "You're up early."

Matthew nodded. "Something smelled good so I came to investigate."

His father always did love breakfast; it was his favorite meal of the day. "How are you feeling?" he asked.

"Better. *Much* better." Matthew held up his cup of coffee as if that had been his cure. "And thanks for making breakfast, Sam."

"You're welcome."

"Hey, what smells so good?" another voice chimed from behind him. Hunter turned to find his brother coming down the stairs at a fast clip.

Hutch was wearing a pair of shorts and another one of his rumpled band T-shirts. Although his eyes were still droopy with sleep and his hair was a mess, he smiled at Sam. "Oh *yes*," he said as she handed him a plate. "Sam makes *the best* breakfasts."

Wait. So no one thought it was weird for her to be here? A glance at Sam told him she was also thinking the same thing. Well, that was a relief. Seemed like his family has come to totally accept her.

"Hey," he said when he caught Owen fooling around with

his food instead of eating. "Hurry up and eat. We're going to be late."

Owen needed no further encouragement. When he saw everyone else digging in with enthusiasm, he picked up his own fork and started eating.

"How do you like it?" Sam asked him.

Owen nodded in answer, his mouth too full to answer. "It's perfect," Hutch answered for him instead. His own mouth was full as he continued to shovel more food into his mouth. "I bet Dacey and Greyson are weeping in their beds right now because they are missing out on this."

"I haven't talked to Dacey since I came home," Matthew said. "Have you?"

Hutch nodded. "Yeah, we've been talking to each other every day."

Really? This was news to him. Since when had they gotten so close?

"Well, in that case, ask her and Greyson to come by later. I want to see her."

"She's already said she was coming by later."

"Good. I can't wait." Matthew turned to Sam. "So, how's work been for you?"

"Got any ghosts to catch?" Hutch teased.

Sam rolled her eyes at his brother's teasing. "No ghosts this time, thank God. But the new case is going well."

Hutch turned to him. "So now that Dad's out of the hospital, what's going to happen at Gleam?"

That was the question that was likely on everyone's mind at the moment and Hunter turned to see his father's reaction. Matthew frowned but didn't comment. "I don't know," Hunter said. "I guess Dad will step back in whenever he's ready, right?"

Although Matthew nodded, he didn't verbally agree and

that put him on alert. Where was the guy who barked orders like a king? So far, Matthew had been pretty silent as he ate. What was he thinking about?

Oh. He was likely thinking about Clive and their friendship and what the latest arrest would do to their bond. Hunter wasn't sure if things were capable of going back to the way they'd been before, but he was still hopeful.

"Um, Hunter?"

He glanced up at Sam, who was giving him a look he couldn't decipher. And then he realized that she was motioning to the clock with her eyes. *"Oh shit!"* It was a quarter to eight! Owen was going to be late! Bolting up, he grabbed Owen and rushed for the door, ignoring the laughter behind him.

Despite the rush he was in, he still managed a thought: *He couldn't wait to come back and spend time with his family.*

Sam headed home after leaving the Hewitt house. While it was likely that more work would pop up and disturb her peace, she wanted to just take a breather for herself.

Now that her sister's wedding had passed, she realized that she had a lot more free time than she'd had before. Maybe now she could go back to her gardening plans in the front yard.

She'd been reminded of it after chatting with Amara last night and, now, she was getting excited all over again. She'd started it because she'd wanted to fit in with her neighbors more but she quickly realized that she enjoyed it too. She loved being able to use her hands and get down and dirty and watch as the lovely flowers bloomed because of her handiwork.

Sam was just about to jump in the shower when her phone rang. "Where are you?" Deacon asked when she answered.

"Just got home. Why?"

"You just got home right now?"

"Yeah. I spent the night at Hunter's." Not that it was any of his business or anything. "Is there a reason for your call? I'm just about to jump in the tub."

"I just wanted to say that you did good." Sam froze. *Wait a minute. Was Deacon Thorpe praising her?* "What made you look into Mickey?" he asked.

"Well, when you came to me with the evidence of the oil stain, I knew someone else had to have been there. There was just no way Clive could've had the time to do it all. Plus, in speaking to Garcia, he informed me that the damage to the brakes had to have been done right before Matthew left. In this case, timing is everything."

Mickey would've had plenty of time to work on the car while Matthew was preoccupied. And if he kicked it, his father would be able to take his spot.

"When we interviewed him," Deacon said. "He said that he'd gone to meet up with a friend. However, interestingly enough, his friend said he didn't see him that night."

"Busted." The guy had no alibi.

"Yup."

Sam smiled as happiness filled her. They'd done it. They'd finally figured out what happened! A streak of pride shot through her. This was why she loved her job so much. It always gave her such an adrenaline kick.

"So what's your plan for the day?" Deacon asked, tone pleased.

"I'm actually going to take the rest of the day off."

"I'm jealous."

"Please, you thrive on the rush." And the guy was married to his job.

"A bit like someone else I know," he drawled. "Anyway, I've got some work to do. I'll talk to you later."

After hanging up, Sam stripped and slid into the warm water. As she lay her head back and relaxed, she pretended it was Hunter's hands running over her body. Just like that, her lust spiked and her heart started to pound. Oh God. If she wasn't careful, she could see herself falling hard for this man.

Hell, she was already half in love with him already. He'd been so gentle with her, and yet, he pushed her limits. She couldn't imagine how much more explosive their night would've been if they'd been alone and could do whatever they wanted.

They still had a ways to go with learning more about each other but they had all the time in the world. And as Sam allowed her mind to go blank, she really couldn't think of anything better than getting to experience it all with him by her side.

TWENTY-ONE

A FTER HER BATH, SAM TOOK A NAP. IT WAS A LUXURY she'd never had the time for before, but after the night she'd had, she certainly needed it. Dozing off in Hunter's arms had been a dream. If only she could stay there forever and bask in the solid warmth of his body. Unfortunately, her sheets and pillow would have to do for now until she could see him again.

She woke only when there was a soft knock on her door. Rising slowly, Sam was surprised to see that it was already late in the afternoon. She must've been more tired than she thought because she'd slept most of the day away. When she reached the door, she found Hunter on the other side. He smiled at her and Sam felt her stomach do a flip. "Hey, can I come in?"

Sam immediately opened the door. "What are you doing here?"

"Been thinking about you all day," Hunter murmured, pulling her in close. He dove in for a kiss, but it wasn't just a kiss that said *I miss you*; it was a kiss that said, *I can't stop thinking about you and I need you right now.*

When Sam pulled away, she was dizzy with breathlessness. "Whoa, that was some kiss."

Hunter's obsidian eyes glinted with mischief. "I could kiss you some more," he offered.

Sam laughed. "Kissing usually gets us into trouble."

"Maybe." He took her hand and led her back to her bedroom. "But it certainly is a lot of fun."

"Where's Owen?" Didn't he need to pick him up?

"He's getting picked up by Hutch."

"Oh, okay." She sat back down on the edge of her bed. "So that means I'm free for the next few hours."

"What do you want to do?"

Leaning forward, Hunter dropped his mouth to hers again. "I've got a few ideas," he whispered against her lips.

She now knew she wasn't the only one who was pining for the other. A wide smile curled her lips as she looked down at his crotch, the evidence that he wanted her just as much as she wanted him. The fabric of his slacks was pulled tightly over his growing erection and Sam yearned to know what it would feel like inside of her.

"Well, what are you waiting for?" she asked when he just stood there gazing down at her.

In answer, Hunter simply reached out and brushed his thumb against her lips. It made her gasp, mainly because she wasn't expecting it. Normally when a man stood before her, they'd waste no time dropping trou, but once again Hunter was slowing things down.

His thumb circled her lips, the touch so soft it felt like a feather. But he continued to gaze down on her with eyes that mesmerized, keeping her in the moment, keeping her with him.

Soon, she was reaching for him, but Hunter stepped back. He didn't stop playing with her lips though and it was making her go crazy. Everyone was right. Hunter Happa-Hewitt was the master of anticipation because now she was more than ready for him to push her into the bed and have his way with her.

But all Hunter did next was dip the tip of his finger into her mouth. Sam quickly latched onto it, sucking hard. Hunter let out a low groan and palmed himself through his slacks. She could see how hard he was by the outline and she couldn't wait to have it in her mouth.

Finally, Hunter began undoing his pants, reaching in to free what Sam wanted the most. Her eyes were riveted to it, and her mouth started to water the longer she stared.

Her hand was much too small to wrap all the way around him but she didn't care. She used two hands to jack him off as he started to remove his tie. "Fuck," Hunter gritted. "That's good."

Yes, her mind chanted. She'd been waiting so long for this moment. She couldn't wait to dive in and indulge. "Yes, baby. Keep going. That's perfect."

His constant encouragements made her even bolder and turned her on even more. So when Hunter grabbed the back of her neck and pushed her hair into a ball in his fist, she was more than ready to taste him.

The moment her tongue touched him, she moaned.

So many nights she would lie in bed and wonder why she hadn't been good enough. With the Army she hadn't been skilled or strong enough. And with her mother . . . well, her mother just never could accept that she wasn't like Serena.

But Hunter never tried to change her, never made her feel inadequate. In fact, since the very first moment she met him, he'd always seen her as more than what she really was. And that was why she felt a greater connection to him than anyone else.

Sam had come to trust him and knew that he'd never do anything to hurt her.

Surprise hit her when Hunter drew his tie around her neck, not choking her with it, but just tightening it enough to give her the sensation of being tied up. She'd never had a thing for bondage before but this with Hunter was turning her on so much that she let out a low moan.

"Yes, that's good. *More.*"

Sam was more than happy to oblige. She took him deeper into her mouth, holding him there and breathing through her nose until she couldn't anymore. Sloppiness had never appealed to her but, again, what was the harm when she felt more alive than ever before.

Soon, Hunter ditched the tie and lowered himself to her. She laughed as Hunter got rid of the rest of his clothes before working on her clothes next. His control was slipping and she intended to unravel him some more.

After quickly rolling on a condom, Hunter spread her legs and dropped a hand between them. "You're so wet."

She couldn't deny it with the way his fingers came away slick. "Hurry," she begged. She couldn't wait any longer. She needed him so much.

But Hunter took his time, entering her inch by slow inch. Sam let her head fall back on a cry as he started a rhythm that drove her insane. "Oh my God." He was destroying every last bit of her control!

She searched his face, hoping to catch a glimpse of those dark, obsidian eyes, but to her surprise, Hunter's gaze was focused on the point where they were joined. A flush crept high on her cheeks in response.

Oh my God, he was watching them! Hunter slammed into her and Sam cried out. Pushing herself up on her elbows, she watched them too. There was something very raw about it, something intimate and animalistic.

A fierce blush crested high on her cheeks right as she let out a scream. Hunter's head snapped up, a demonic smile splitting his face before he took hold of her legs and slammed into her.

Pleasure hit her from all sides. As she fisted the sheets and screamed at the ceiling, Hunter pounded into her. Sam flew into a second orgasm, which was just as intense as the first. Hunter quickly followed her, shuddering in her arms as she clutched at him.

"Holy shit," he rasped as he slumped back onto the bed. "I've never come that hard in my entire life."

"I haven't either," she admitted.

Must've been all that pent-up energy. She was surprised she hadn't gone off like a rocket within the first five minutes.

"I'm starving," Hunter stated after he caught his breath.

"Did you have lunch?"

"I had a salad, but that's about it. I didn't get a chance to get anything before I came here."

A smile spread over her lips. "You rushed here after work so you could get laid?"

Hunter grinned at her, completely unrepentant. "You say it like I should be ashamed of myself."

"No, never be ashamed of that. Come on." She got up and quickly cleaned herself off in the bathroom. "Want me to make you something to eat?"

Hunter rose and followed her. "A small snack is fine. Don't bother going all out for me."

But she found that she wanted to. If she was going to go all out for anyone, it would be him, the man who made her feel like a sexy woman.

Hunter was in heaven. Ever since his divorce, he felt like he was running on fumes, but now that everything had been cleared up concerning his father and his accident, he felt like he could finally relax. Not to mention he'd just had some explosive sex with Sam.

Good sex always seemed to put him in a good mood, but Hunter felt more cheery than usual. It had to be Sam. She had a special way of bringing out the happiness in him. Whether it was getting him to relax after a stressful day or watching her play with his son, Sam always managed to bring a smile to his face.

He'd quickly put on his boxers and headed for the kitchen. He could already smell something amazing and his stomach growled in approval.

Far be it for him to tell Sam what to do. Instead of fixing up a simple snack, she looked to be making a full-course meal in the kitchen.

His hunger for food, however, was quickly overtaken by another kind of hunger when he realized that Sam had put on his dress shirt. He'd never seen anything hotter in his entire life.

She was all sleek lines and beautiful curves. The sight of her slim legs on display made him think of how they'd feel wrapped around his waist as he drove into her.

"Hunter!" she squeaked as he wrapped his arms around her. "What are you doing? I can't cook like this!"

"Forget about the food," he growled. "I need you again."

"But—"

She was silenced when he started scattering her neck with kisses. They made her laugh, which was just what he intended. He turned her around so she was facing him and cupped her cheek. "Your smile brings me so much joy."

A fierce blush spread across her cheeks. It was a magnificent sight.

Reaching past her, he turned off the stove. "Hunter!"

"Shh." Lifting her leg up, he wrapped it around his waist before quickly slapping on another condom. If Sam didn't want him, she would've pushed him away. Instead, she drew her hands up over his chest and hooked them behind his neck.

"You're quite the distraction, you know."

"Sorry." He wasn't sorry at all. He entered her smoothly, groaning as he seated himself deep.

Fuck. He would never get enough of this.

Sam Cosi had him wrapped around her little finger and he wouldn't have it any other way. In an attempt to steady herself, Sam propped herself against the countertop. Once he was sure she was comfortable, he set a brutal pace that sent them both soaring.

Never in a million years did he think he'd end up here with Sam. He'd only come to her out of concern for his father, but she had proven to him that she was smarter than all the rest. This amazing woman had come into his life because of unusual circumstances, but he wouldn't have changed anything despite the stress and anxiety that had come with it.

He pulled out and turned Sam around. In this position, she was bent over the countertop. He propped one of her legs up too before sliding into her again.

"Oh, Hunter. That feels so good!"

He could only grunt in agreement. Now she could push down on him, taking him deeper. He also now had the perfect view of her back tattoo.

He touched it now, gingerly at first, learning the lines of her beautiful body before his grip tightened. When Sam cried out, he knew he'd found the spot that would make her scream his name. Shit. He hoped he wasn't being too rough with her. Sometimes when he got lost in the moment like this, he got a little uncontrolled. He forced himself to loosen his hold.

"No, don't! Come on," she demanded. Gone was the girl with the beautiful flush. The tough girl was showing again and he fucking loved it. As Sam continued to urge him on, his control unraveled. His legs shook and sweat poured from his body, but he wasn't going to stop until Sam came.

He pounded into her until a keening whine filled the air. And then, he lost it too, pouring all the love he had for her into her until he felt like he blacked out.

It wasn't until Sam pushed him off her and kissed him again that he felt his world return to him. Hell, after this, *Sam* was his world.

"What the hell would I do without you?" he rasped before dropping his mouth to hers.

TWENTY-TWO

S AM HAD JUST FINISHED UP ANOTHER CASE AND WAS ON her way home when she received a call from Hunter. "Hey, baby. Where are you?"

"I'm in my car on my way home. Why?" She knew him well enough now to catch when something was up.

"It's Owen. We have swimming lessons today but he suddenly doesn't want to go."

"Oh no, has he been acting differently again?"

"He seemed fine earlier but maybe he's just nervous."

"What can I do to help?"

"Do you mind meeting us there? Maybe seeing you will calm him down."

"Of course." But Sam hardly doubted that her presence alone would do the trick. She knew all about nerves and how detrimental they could be to physical performance. Hopefully by having them both there Owen would be reassured that nothing was going to happen to him.

Fifteen minutes later, Sam found herself standing in front of the recreation center. "I'm so glad you came," Hunter said as he approached, carrying Owen in his arms. He quickly kissed her on the lips but the effect was enough to have her body burning for him.

"I'm glad too," she returned. "And how are you doing, little man?" She turned to face Owen, who had his face burrowed into Hunter's neck. She would've thought it cute if she didn't know how distressed he was. With a finger, she poked him gently, hoping to get him to smile but her own smile faded when she saw tears spring in his eyes. "Aw, what's wrong?"

"He's a little nervous," Hunter said.

"It'll be fine." They walked inside together. Sam's hand gripped Owen's tightly, trying to reassure him that he wasn't alone. Trying something new was always a little scary but Owen was a smart kid. He'd get the hang of it quickly.

For a moment, they scanned the pool. Several other kids were already in the water, all wearing safety gear to keep them safe. Dotted around the perimeter were several lifeguards and instructors, all ready to help in case something when wrong. Sam was sure that nothing was going to happen but she was still a little nervous for Owen. "Do you want to try going in?" she asked him. Hunter tried to put him down on the floor, but it seemed that he was having trouble unlatching his kid from him. Sam laughed. "Okay, how about we watch for a bit?"

They sat down at the edge of the pool, watching as some of the other kids played. "Hey, you know what?" Hunter said. "Why don't I go in first?"

"Good idea." If Owen saw it, maybe he wouldn't be so afraid to go in. Sam could already see that several other parents were in the water with their kids, so she didn't see the harm.

Hunter slid into the water, making sure to stay close to Owen. "The water is nice. Want to try it?"

Owen shook his head.

"Is there a problem here?" a man asked. Sam looked up into the eyes of one of the young instructors.

"Ah, sorry. We're just dealing with some nerves here."

"Don't worry. This happens quite a lot with first-timers." He bent down to Owen's eye level. "Are you sure you want to just sit here? It's a whole lot of fun once you're in the water."

There was no response from Owen however. He simply

stared down at his hands, which still gripped his shorts tightly.

"Thanks," Sam said, brushing a hand over Owen's head to comfort him. "Maybe we'll just dip our toes in this time."

"Sounds great." As the instructor rose and left, Sam turned to Hunter again.

"How about you come in the water?" he suggested.

Sam shook her head. "Can't. I don't have a change of clothes."

"Normally naked would be fine with me," he teased. "But I don't want the other dads here getting the wrong idea."

Laughing, Sam shook her head and splashed him with a handful of water. "You're crazy."

The water hit him right in the face. "Ah! Stop!" Hunter cried as he flinched away.

To her surprise, Owen laughed.

Hunter's eyes narrowed at his kid. "You like that, huh? What if I did that to you?" He motioned splashing Owen with water and he flinched but no water had actually hit him.

Owen balked. "Huh?"

"Gotcha." That playful smile Sam loved on Hunter was in place. And so was the mischievous glint in his dark eyes. She loved this look on him and she especially loved watching him interact with his son. It was both sexy and sweet to see his patience come through in his parenting.

"How about we do what Sam suggested and take off these shoes?" Hunter said now. "It'd be nice to feel the water on your feet."

Again surprising her, Owen nodded and Hunter immediately began removing his shoes. When he caught her looking, he said, "You too."

"Me?"

"Yup. Get them off. If Owen is doing it, you have to, too."

Owen nodded at her in agreement.

"Oh, fine." On a sigh, she shucked off her boots and set them to the side. "Ready?" she asked Owen as she kept her feet up in the air. "One . . . two . . . *three!*"

They both dunked their feet in at the same time, creating a big splash that hit Hunter again. "Hey! You guys!" he snarled.

Owen laughed again. Seeing that smile on his face made all the waiting worth it. "So what do you think?" she asked as she kicked her feet in the water. "Feels nice, right?"

"Yeah."

"Feel like jumping in?" Hunter prompted. Owen quickly shook his head. "Okay, we'll stick with this for a while."

As she and Owen practiced kicking their legs, she felt him start to relax. She never thought that spending the afternoon in a pool surrounded by kids would be a source of fun for her but Sam was quickly realizing just how much she enjoyed spending time with these two.

Not only was it a treat to watch this sinfully sexy man encourage and comfort his son, but she also loved getting the chance to spend time with his incredibly brilliant kid. Owen had quickly become one of her favorite people.

"Hey!" she cried when Hunter suddenly splashed them. "Don't get me wet. I don't have a change of clothes!"

Owen laughed as the water quickly soaked into her clothes.

Annoyance ignited, Sam kicked at the water and sent a wave in Hunter's direction. It was a bull's-eye hit but since he was already wet, it didn't hold the same impact.

"*Dammit.*"

With the hour coming to an end, many of the other families and instructors were going home, leaving them alone in the pool. "Are you guys going to be okay here?" another one of the instructors asked.

"Yeah. Do you mind if we stay a little bit longer?" Hunter asked him. When it looked like he was going to refuse, he added, "Five minutes."

"Okay, fine. Five minutes only."

"Thank you."

Hunter turned his attention back to his kid. "You heard him. Five minutes! Feel like going in for a quick dip?"

While he didn't outright refuse, Owen didn't say yes either. Hunter held his arms out, his expression bright and encouraging. "Come on, I'll be holding you the entire time. And Sam will be here too."

The kid looked over at her, as if to make sure she was really there. Sam reached out and rested her hand on his shoulder. "It'll be okay. Go and have some fun."

Something must've clicked because Owen nodded and allowed Hunter to pull him in. He held him close, making sure not to scare him off by going in too deep but enough that most of his body was wet.

"Do you like it?" she called out.

Owen nodded and even reached out to touch the surface of the water with his hands. He made a big splash and laughed when the water hit Hunter in the face.

God, they were so cute together. Something inside of her chest tightened as a smile burst across her face. She was silly to think that she'd one day fall in love with them because the truth was, she was already.

Sam cared for them a great deal and if something were to happen to either of them, she wouldn't know what she'd do. "You should come in," Hunter said, pulling her in from her thoughts.

"You know I can't. I don't have a change of clothes!"

"You're wearing underwear, right?"

"Hunter!"

He chuckled. "Okay, okay." Instead Sam sat on the edge of the pool, watching father and son play in the water. For the entire time, she smiled, actually wishing that she'd brought an extra change of clothes so that she could join them.

When Hunter finally brought back Owen to her side, she asked, "So how was it? Did you have fun?"

Owen nodded. "Daddy said we could come back next week."

Her heart exploded at the excitement in his eyes. "That's wonderful."

"Will you come too?"

"Huh?" She was so surprised by the question that it took her a moment to answer. "Of course, darling. I'll be here!"

"Yay!" Owen pounced on her, forgetting the fact that he hadn't yet toweled off. Sam hugged him tightly despite the fact that her clothes were getting wet.

Hunter appeared beside them with a towel. "Let's get you dried off. I'm pretty sure that guy will return to make sure we're gone."

As he rubbed Owen dry and dressed him again, Sam watched on fondly. She had a busy week coming up with some exciting things happening but at the top of the list was getting to spend more time with Owen and Hunter.

Once Owen was dressed again, Hunter reached for her.

"Hey, stay away from me. You're gonna get me all wet."

His dark eyes flashed bright. "That's the plan."

Oh no, she knew that look. She was on her feet before he could reach for her, but he still managed to catch her by the waist and bring her back to his body. She squealed as wetness seeped through her clothes. *"Nooo!"* Hunter chuckled in her ear. "I hate you so much."

"Hey, you weren't complaining when Owen was hugging you."

"But he's a cute kid, you're—" His brow rose as he dared her to continue but Sam found that she couldn't. She had nothing at all to complain about when his arms were around her.

She said it before she could lose courage. "I love you, you know that?"

Surprise flashed over his features before his eyes darkened. He pulled her tighter against him. "I love you too. Thank you for being here."

Their kiss was soft and sweet but it had the same effect of an avalanche; it shook her to her core. When she pulled away, she was gasping.

But Hunter had to totally ruin the moment when he gave one hard tug to her arm and she fell into the pool. Instinctively, she reached out, pulling him down with her. They hit the water in a splash.

"Daddy!" Owen yelled but he seemed relieved as they came back up to the surface. Sputtering, Sam wiped her hair from her face before her enraged gaze landed on Hunter.

He was on the other side of the pool already, laughing his head off. "I can't believe you did that!" she screamed.

Pulling herself out of the pool, Sam tried to remove as much of the water from her clothes as she could. She also noticed that Owen was quietly smiling beside her, trying hard not to laugh.

Hunter rounded the pool and returned to her side. She noticed that he was staying a good distance away from her though. When she shot him a death glare, he mumbled a "sorry," but he didn't look the least bit sorry at all. In fact, he looked smug. Finally, he picked up Owen and carried him to her. "You're too fun to leave alone," he said by way of explanation.

Sam felt her annoyance leave her. She leaned in until their foreheads touched. "Then don't ever leave me."

Hunter's grip tightened around her. "I won't."

That moment would've been perfect if not for the fact that her clothes were all sticking to her body. Sam made a face as she pulled the damp fabric from her body.

That was when Owen started to laugh, and as punishment, she tickled him on his side until he was laughing uncontrollably. Soon they were all laughing, and Sam forgot all about being drenched with water.

Soaked or not, she was just going to enjoy this moment with two of her favorite people.

TWENTY-THREE

THIS WAS THE MOONRISE BEACH HE KNEW AND LOVED. In the last few weeks, Hunter hadn't had much time to really enjoy the beautiful scenery around him. He'd been too preoccupied with caring for Owen and his father that personal enjoyment took a back seat. However, now that everything was behind them, he was going to take the advice that Sam had said to him all those days ago and have a day solely for him.

Well, him *and* her.

After she'd dropped everything for him and Owen the other day, he wanted to repay her somehow. But he knew that Sam would balk at anything he'd give her, so instead of showering her with gifts, he was going to take her someplace he knew she'd love.

He hadn't told her what he had planned, just that she dress for the beach. She was going to be in for a nice surprise when she realized what they were going to do today.

When he pulled up to her house, she was already waiting outside for him and Hunter had to take a moment and pick his jaw up from the floor.

Sam looked stunning in a pale yellow sundress that hit her just at the knees. Her shoulders were bare, showing off her new tan and tattoos. And she was smiling at him as he approached.

"Nice shoes." She was wearing a pair of Birks. A lot of women wore them around here. But he didn't figure they were Sam's style.

"Thanks. Dacey gifted them to me."

Ah, that made more sense. His sister had a very distinct taste in fashion and Sam still managed to rock the shoes like a supermodel.

Dropping his head to her, Hunter gave her a long, lingering kiss. "Where's Owen?" Sam asked.

"He's hanging with my dad. It's just going to be you and me today."

"Really?"

"Yup. Is that okay? I thought we needed some alone time together."

"Absolutely. And stop looking at me like that. It's just a dress."

"A very sexy, very *tight* dress." He couldn't help but run his hands over her hips. He loved that she was tall because she could stand head to head to him and he could kiss her anytime he wanted. When she rolled her eyes at him, he shot her a wolfish smile and led her back to the car. "How do you expect me to drive with you beside me looking like that?"

Sam's eyes glinted with amusement. "If this revs you up, wait 'til you see my bikini underneath."

Hunter nearly swallowed his tongue. "You're killing me here, you know that?"

As he pulled out of her driveway and started in the direction opposite the beach, Sam frowned. "Where are we going?"

His grin broadened. "It's a surprise."

Turned out, Sam *loved* surprises because she wouldn't stop pestering him with questions. She reminded him of Owen when he got excited about something "A clue," she pressed. "Just give me *one* clue."

"Nope. I'm not saying anything." He wanted to keep her in the dark until the very end.

"Oh, come on! Now you're just being mean."

He had to laugh. "Just sit back and enjoy the view. We're almost there." He could already see the water and if Sam hadn't figured out what they were going to do, she would in a minute.

As soon as she saw the boats, she turned to him. "Are we going sailing?"

"Yes."

Sam clapped her hands together. "Oh my God! I can't wait!" Fuck, she was cute. "I've never been sailing before!"

"I'm glad to be your first," he drawled, which earned him a slap on the arm.

He was just glad that he could do this for her. Hunter got the feeling that not a lot of people did a lot for Sam. Why would they need to when she was so self-sufficient? Plus, Sam wasn't the kind of woman who you bought flowers for. She deserved a whole lot more.

"So which boat are we taking? Where are we going to go? Do you even know how to operate something like this?"

He had to laugh at the nonstop questions. "Relax, it's going to be great."

She shot him a winning smile. "I'm just glad that we both know how to swim."

"I've had a lot of experience sailing, so I know what I'm doing." He proved it to her when just a few minutes later, they got out of the car and headed to the boat they were going to be using. Hunter had it ready to go in no time and Sam stared at him in awe when he held his hand out for her. "Ready to go?"

"Is this boat yours?"

"No." He only wished it was. "It actually belongs to a friend." Being the CEO of a big company had its perks.

Sam canted her head at the basket that he carried in his other hand. "What have you got in there?"

"Just some snacks for later." He planned on spending the entire day out on the water as long as the weather permitted it. "Better put on some sunscreen. You don't want to burn."

As Sam went to fetch some, he quickly went behind the wheel. Having done this a few times before, Hunter knew exactly where to go but that had been on a smaller boat with only his family aboard. This boat was much nicer with an outside cockpit that was open and spacious, so it would be great for watching the sun go down. It also had a nice foredeck, which was perfect for sunbathing and the dorm-sized kitchen would be more than enough for him and Sam during their stay. Hunter was already anticipating the quality time he'd have with her. And with the sun overhead, they'd be able to enjoy every bit of fantastic elements around them.

Man, this was the life. For once he didn't have to worry about anything. It was a luxury he hadn't been able to afford before. For a while, he just allowed himself to enjoy his time out in the sun and the peaceful tranquility of being out in the water.

When he was satisfied with their position, he turned back to Sam. "Sam, are you hungry? I can make—" He stopped short and promptly lost his ability to breathe.

Holy hell. She'd taken off her dress and was now only wearing a bikini. In pure white, the little triangles spiked his lust into overdrive. Beneath the heavy sun, her skin glowed and it took all of his restraint not to jump on her like he wanted. He was already feeling himself growing hard for her. *Damn, this woman had him wrapped around her little finger.*

Sam smiled up at him, completely oblivious to the reaction she'd caused in him. "What did you say?"

Hunter dropped down beside her and kissed her, unable to help himself. "I said I can make something for us to eat."

"Sure. That sounds great." Sam grinned. "You know, you look like a pro driving this thing but"—she plucked at his T-shirt—"you're going to get a funny-looking tan if you don't take this off."

He shot her a wolfish smile. "If you want me to take my clothes off, just ask."

With a roll of her eyes, she swatted him before handing him a bottle of sunscreen. "Do my back," she ordered.

Oh man. She wanted him to rub her down? In that case, lunch was going to be delayed for sure. He was already having a hard time not looking at her smooth skin. *Touching* it was going to kill him.

Dispensing some of the cream into his palm, he rubbed his hands together before slathering it over her shoulders. Her skin was warm to the touch and when a soft breeze rolled by, it carried her sweet scent to his nostrils.

"That feels good." Sam groaned when he slid his hands down lower on her back to her tiny waist. It'd be so easy to tug on one of the strings of her bikini and watch as the fabric unraveled from her body. Inside his shorts, he felt himself grow harder and he had to grit his teeth from groaning out loud.

Sam glanced at him over her shoulder. "Are you okay?"

No, he wasn't. He was going to come in his shorts if he kept this up. Pulling away, Hunter adjusted himself discreetly before reaching for the basket of food. "Want a drink?" He certainly needed one after *that.*

"Sure. What do you have?" Sam leaned forward and peeked into the bag.

"I have some fruit. Cheese. Wine."

"I'll definitely have some of the wine."

"Wine, it is." As he popped the cap off and poured her a glass, their eyes met and held.

"I can't believe you did this all for me."

"Who else am I going to spoil?" he shot back. Sam deserved to be pampered and treated like a queen.

With a smile on her face, Sam leaned back, tilting her head so that the sun hit her face. "No one has ever gone through so much effort for me," she admitted. "I love it."

Hunter had to force himself to stay put. As revved up as he was, he also loved to just stare at her.

He could watch her like that, all spread out like a queen, but then he reached over and caressed her cheek. Sam closed her fist over his and pounced on him, burrowing herself in his arms. Hunter immediately pulled her in closer to him.

He used to curse his own luck. After the injury that had ended his football career, Hunter went through life without really caring about what happened to himself. But after his divorce, he became a man who worried too much. Being with Sam was helping him find that balance between the two.

They stayed like that for a while, simply enjoying each other's closeness when Sam ran a finger over his shoulders. "You're burning a little bit here."

Oh shit. He'd totally forgotten about reapplying sunscreen. He pulled back and grinned down at her. "If I turned red like a lobster, would you still walk around beside me?"

Sam's laughter lit up her entire face. "Now there's a picture." She leaned in, brushing her lips against his. "But you're going to have to do more than that to get rid of me."

"It's my big boat, isn't it," he drawled.

Sam laughed again. "Actually. It's this . . ." Her hand had found his hard length trapped between them. He groaned loudly as she began to stroke him through his shorts. Thank God there was no one around to hear him. In fact, he was glad that there was no one around at all. They could do whatever the hell they wanted without being heard or seen.

Sam flashed him a wicked grin before she started on his zipper and dropped to her knees.

"*Oh fuck.*" This was really happening. When her mouth wrapped around the head of his cock, he let out a long moan.

From between his legs, Sam gazed up at him, her tongue darting out to lick a line up his cock. "Fuck, you're gorgeous," he rasped, touching her swollen lips.

She worked him good, taking him down as far as she could. Each time he used his hand to guide her. As she continued to destroy all his thoughts, Hunter could only hold on for dear life.

"Should I take my bikini off?" Sam was already pushing apart the cups of her top so that her beautiful little breasts were exposed to the sun.

"The bottoms," he rasped. "Just the bottoms."

With a smile, Sam straightened and tugged on the string at her hip, unraveling herself like a prize. Hunter stopped breathing altogether. "*Holy shit.* Come here."

He ran his hands down her beautiful legs and eased her thighs further apart. Once again, he was glad for the privacy they had. He didn't want anyone else seeing Sam like this. This would only be for his eyes alone.

As she leaned back and got comfortable, his gaze latched onto her center. She was pink and perfect and glistening already for him and, man, did he want to dive in. Unable to resist himself, Hunter dipped down and tasted her sweetness.

He teased her until Sam cried out. And then he added a finger to give her more, loving the way she tipped her head back and let out a groan. God, she was tight. And she was drenched too. He could easily fit another finger. So he did. "You like that?"

"Yes. Don't stop."

Oh, he was just getting started.

Taking her clit into his mouth, he moved his fingers inside of her. Sam gasped and pulled his hair, telling him exactly what she wanted. He loved that about her, that she wasn't shy about her needs. In seconds, tremors racked her body and Hunter watched her detonate.

Her orgasm was swift and intense, making her tremble in his arms. And as she came back down to him, Hunter simply held her. "Wow. That was amazing." Hunter leaned back in and kissed her, savoring the heat swirling around them.

Sam laughed in a burst. "You might want to do something about that." He looked down to where she was looking. His cock was sticking out like a flagpole as if it say, *hey, what about me?*

"What do you want?" she asked. Just like that, she was game again.

"Get on your hands and knees." He wanted to fuck her from behind.

Sam immediately complied, even going so far as to wiggle her ass at him. Chuckling, he gave it a little swat before rolling a condom on. Then he was pushing in slowly. *"Oh God."*

The slow glide was heaven and hell rolled into one. He wanted nothing more than to pound into her but instead he took his time, wanting nothing more than to make the moment last forever. He held still for a long moment, taking it all in.

It was only when Sam demanded that he move that he started rocking his hips.

A string of expletives flew from her lips as he increased pace. Sam had to grip the boat in front of her as it started to rock.

Pressure built in his balls, cresting higher and higher until he had to grit his teeth to keep from coming. Seconds later, Sam was coming around him, her pussy convulsing and throwing him over. He let out a shout as he came, feeling it go on and on. He had no idea how long it was until he opened his eyes again.

When he did though, Sam was watching him over her shoulder. "Damn," he muttered. He hadn't expected *that.*

He quickly got rid of the condom and returned to her side. Sam was still smiling at him. "Why do you keep looking at me like that?"

"It's nothing." She leaned forward and nuzzled his ear. "But you are getting a little burnt."

Hunter kissed her again. "It was worth it," he whispered. Sunburned or not, nothing was going to make him forget this epic day.

Sam's smile brightened. "In that case, do you want some more wine?"

"Oh yeah."

TWENTY-FOUR

AFTER THAT WONDERFUL DAY OFF WITH HUNTER, SAM had to return to work the next day. She'd been working all day in her office when an unexpected visitor knocked on her door.

Through the window, she could see the silhouette of a tall, broad figure. Who would this person be? She wasn't expecting anyone. "Come in," she called out.

Her visitor poked his head through but didn't fully walk in. "Hi. Are—are you Sam Cosi?"

"I am." Sam didn't recognize this man. Her time working as a private investigator had helped her hone her reading skills. Now she was usually able to tell a lot about a person with just one glance.

She thought about what she might look like to him. Although people told her she was pretty when she smiled, her expression was pinched with suspicion as she looked up at this stranger. Something about him felt off to her but she still couldn't pinpoint why.

Now that she'd announced herself, the man seemed more comfortable and stepped through the door, closing it behind him. He looked to be in his mid-twenties but she wasn't so sure because his hair was left so long that several strands covered most of his face from her gaze.

He wore a navy blazer and dark blue jeans. She figured that had been his effort to look presentable this morning. He reminded her a lot of those preppy kids she used to hate in college. "My name is Phillip Charms," he said.

Sam rose, walked around her desk and extended her hand. "It's nice to meet you, Mr. Charms. Can I help you with something?" Why was this kid looking for her?

"It—it's about Mickey," he stammered.

Sam's smile vanished in an instant. *What the hell?* "What about Mickey?" The man had already been charged with his involvement in Matthew's accident. When Phillip remained silent, Sam felt her anger start to rise. "What do you know?" she asked again. Phillip looked visibly distressed and now that she was standing closer to him, she could see that his eyes were bloodshot and his skin was clammy. He looked very uneasy and Sam decided then that she didn't like this man. He was going to ruin her day. *"Tell me!"*

Phillip jumped at her voice. "Okay, okay! I just wanted to say that Mickey didn't do it."

Sam's world did a fast tilt. *"Excuse me?"*

"Mickey didn't do it," he repeated. "He didn't try to kill that guy."

"But there's evidence against him. He has motive and he didn't have an alibi." How could it not have been him? "Wait." She gave her head a furious shake. "How do you—"

And then it hit her who this man was.

Seeing that she caught on, Phillip nodded. "He was with me the whole night."

"But didn't the police question you?"

"I lied," he confessed. When Sam opened her mouth to yell at him, Phillip flinched. "I panicked, okay? I didn't know what to do and I just sort of—" He broke off as his voice cracked. "I didn't realize this was going to happen to him!"

The pressure in her temples increased. *Dammit!* Why the hell did these kids think it was okay to lie to the police? Sam closed her eyes and rubbed her temples with a hand. "Why are you telling me this?" Shouldn't he have gone to the police? How did he find her?

"I don't know," he admitted. "I guess I'm afraid. Mickey told me about you. Said you were a bit mean, but that you were smart."

"He said that?"

Phillip nodded. "I don't know what to do. I thought maybe you could help me."

Aw fuck. He was likely feeling guilty for what Mickey was going through. But if she found out that he was lying and he was just trying to get his friend off the hook, there would be dangerous consequences.

"Tell me everything that happened that night," Sam ordered. "No more lies. No more avoiding the question."

Phillip sighed. "I invited Mickey over to my house. It's in Palm Harbor." Sam noted that that was about an hour drive away. Phillip took a breath. "We got high on mushrooms and then Mickey stayed the night."

Holy fucking hell. Sam shook her head, trying to wrap her head around all this. "Why didn't you say anything before?"

"I'm up for a scholarship to this really big school. I thought that if they found out or if my parents knew, it would blow my chances of getting in."

This just kept getting more and more messed up. "Why haven't you gone to the police with this?" If what Phillip was saying was true, then the police had just arrested the wrong fucking guy!

"I don't know. I guess I'm scared about what's going to happen."

"I'm sorry, kid, but we have to go to the police with this." She grabbed her jacket with one hand and clamped the other on the kid's shoulder, turning him toward the door. Deacon would probably shit a brick when he learned of this news. Hell, with this disastrous turn of events, he'd probably shit a cinder block! Everything was so fucked up.

Phillip took a step but then stopped abruptly. Sam could only arch her brow in response. If he fought, or if he tried to run away, she'd be forced to take him down. He now had information that the police needed to hear. "Wait." His voice sounded shaky and unstable. "What's going to happen to me?"

"That's for the police to decide," she answered before giving him a hard shove.

* * *

Sam hated going to the Moonrise Beach Police Station mainly because a lot of the guys liked to tease her about Deacon. They were always going on about going out with him but Sam always thought that it was a ridiculous notion. She and Deacon were strictly friends, and although he had shown an interest in her and asked her out a few times, she'd always told him no. That never stopped his colleagues from trying to persuade her though.

"Hey, Sam!" Juliana called out as she walked through the doors. "It's been a while. How have you been?"

Another cop came forward and shot her a smile. "Sam, are you here to see Deacon?" He waggled his brows at her and winked.

She just resisted flipping him off. "As a matter of fact, I am. Can you call him for me?"

Juliana stepped beside her, her earlier friendly disposition gone as she recognized the guy with her. "Wait a minute. What's going on here? What are you doing here?" she asked Phillip.

The kid beside her looked pale as a ghost and seemed to be struggling with his words so Sam answered for him. "He's got some explaining to do. It's really important that we see Deacon."

"I'm right here."

At the sound of her friend's voice, Sam turned. Deacon was in his usual uniform, actually looking pretty good despite the shadows beneath his eyes. But those eyes weren't focused on her; they were locked on Phillip as he approached. "What the hell is going on? Why is he here?"

Sam presented Phillip to him. "This gentleman here lied to you." She watched as Deacon's face went from shocked to angry. "He wasn't truthful about the events that happened the night of the accident. So I suggest you get him in a room right now and redo that interview."

"Son of a bitch!" Juliana cursed. "Are you serious?"

Perhaps she should've felt bad for dropping the bomb like that, but a lesson had to be learned where Phillip was concerned. Maybe next time he wouldn't lie to the police.

Lips curling, Deacon only snarled as he took hold of Phillips's arm and turned for the interview room. He paused only for a moment to say, "I'll talk to you later."

Oooh, he was pissed.

Sam would've smiled if this whole situation wasn't so fucked up already.

While Deacon was usually pretty easygoing and fun, he took his job *very* seriously. Something like this was a setback he didn't need, and Sam didn't want to be around when he exploded.

As soon as they were out of sight, she let out a breath of frustration. She hated this. How the fuck did her day go from pleasant to complete shit within minutes? Also, she felt partly responsible for all this. After all, she'd been the one who had suspected something was going on with Mickey. And now there was a chance that Mickey wasn't the guy they'd been looking for! *Oh God.* What was she going to tell Hunter?

But if Mickey *and* Clive hadn't done it, then who had?

Hunter sat in his car of Owen's school's parking lot, checking over his emails on his smartphone. He'd left work earlier to come and pick him up. They had a dentist appointment to go to and Hunter hated being late. But now that he had some extra time to kill, he decided to call Sam and see how she was doing.

The phone rang and rang but she didn't pick up. Frowning, he wondered what she was doing. Hopefully she was okay and wasn't having another one of those stressful days.

Now that his father was back on his feet, he knew his days at Gleam were numbered. Hunter still wasn't exactly sure what to think about it all. Although he hadn't wanted the job initially, he was now finding it quite enjoyable. Even with everything going on, the workers had accepted him easily and Hunter realized that he was going to miss a lot of them when he left.

Owen seemed to fall into the rhythm of things too. The anxiety he'd been feeling earlier seemed to be diminishing with each day. He wasn't sure if that was due to him just getting used to things or if it was because he had a greater support group to help him, but it made Hunter happy to see him doing better. As of right now, his family was tighter than ever. Dacey and Greyson visited the house nearly every week now and no one had had a fight in weeks. It was miraculous how far they'd come from before. He was glad for it. For once, they were truly acting like a family.

Although Owen hadn't mentioned wanting his mother again since his breakdown at school, Hunter still wouldn't forget it. Hopefully, he wasn't missing her as much now that he had the rest of their family to lean on.

As he got out of the car to wait by the door, he tried calling Sam again. Again, the phone rang but no one answered. *Please don't be doing anything dangerous.* He wouldn't be able to handle it if something happened to her.

He was just about to text her when a figure stepped before him. Glancing up, Hunter was horrified to find the woman of his past standing behind him. "What the—"

His ex-wife looked like a female version of Johnny Cash in head to toe black. The patent pumps she wore made her look taller than she really was, and this time, she'd put waves in her hair. Hunter shot her a confused look. "What are you doing here?" He probably hadn't seen her for months. Not since their divorce was finalized and they'd gone their separate ways. She hadn't even bothered to come see her own son on his birthday. So what the hell was she doing here now? "Are you here to see Owen?"

"No. I actually came to see you."

"Why?" *What the hell did she want from him?*

"I wanted to see how things were going with you."

"But why do you care?" She hadn't cared about him when she'd cheated on him with that young barista she'd left him for.

"Oh, come on. Don't be like that, Hunter. We were together once."

"Yeah, but we aren't anymore," he shot back. He wasn't under any illusions either.

As his ex closed the distance between them, Hunter felt his panic start to rise. What if Owen walked out of school right this moment and saw him talking to her? Would he be glad to see her or would he remember the betrayal he was currently feeling right now?

Once Hunter got full custody of his kid, he'd vow to himself that he would do everything to protect his child. He wouldn't allow any harm to come to him, and that included protecting him from his mother.

He still couldn't believe that his *ex-wife* was standing before him! She still looked beautiful, he'd give her that, but that sweet agony he used to feel when he'd look at her was no longer there. Now all he felt when he looked into her blue eyes was bleak darkness. She was a black hole and he wasn't going to allow himself to get sucked in again. He had to get rid of her and send her away before Owen saw her. "Chrissy, you need to leave."

"Why? Can't we talk for a little bit?"

Hunter shook his head. "No. We can't."

"Why not?"

"Because I don't want to talk to you."

"Well, that's a little harsh."

"I'm sorry if I hurt your feelings but you and I know you've done more harm to me than I have to you."

Her mouth dropped open like he'd slapped her. "I was just trying to be nice!"

"Why bother? There's nothing you can do to make me forgive you." He'd trusted her and she had betrayed him. "What's done is done." He had moved on already and he had no intention of every looking back. He wasn't going to make a fool of himself again. "Please leave us alone."

Chrissy's bottom lip trembled before she looked away. "You're such an asshole," she snarled before stomping off.

Hunter could only sigh in relief when she disappeared

from his sight. He still had no idea what prompted Chrissy to come seek him out, but he was just glad that Owen hadn't been around to see her. But now that his guards were up, he was wary of everything around him. Only when he could guarantee that she would never try to speak to them again would be finally be able to relax.

TWENTY-FIVE

S AM HEADED STRAIGHT BACK TO HER OFFICE TO COMPOSE herself. This shit was getting ridiculous! She'd never had a case that had thrown her so off course before. How could she have suspected two people wrongly? She felt like they were no closer to finding out the truth of what really happened that night than when she'd first started.

God, how was she going to face Hunter again? Even worse, how was she going to explain all this to Matthew? She'd promised him the next time he'd see her she'd have it all figured out. But it seemed that everyone was either lying or telling her and the police only bits of the truth. With such big gaps in the story, how was she ever going to figure everything out?

She felt terrible for ignoring Hunter's calls earlier but she still hadn't figured out what she was going to say. Maybe once Deacon was done questioning Phillip again, he'd call her and tell her what their next plan of action would be. She just didn't want to worry Hunter more than she needed.

Despite her growing headache, Sam decided she would go back to the beginning and map out the events she knew to be true. After work, Matthew had driven to Clive's house to have dinner with him. They'd talked about work and their colleagues, including Brian Melwood and an argument they'd had earlier. At the time, neither she nor the police knew that Mickey had moved back temporarily with his father.

But Mickey had gone to Palm Harbor that night to Phillip Charms's house. That meant he had had to have left the house before Matthew had in order to reach Phillip's house. Now the question was, how did a stain appear on Clive's car if Mickey had taken the car with him? It just didn't make any sense.

Sam shook her head. Maybe something had been knocked loose and was preventing her from thinking clearly. She was obviously missing something. But what was it?

Pulling out her original suspect list, she went through it once again. Both Diego Garcia, the mechanic, and Brian Melwood, Matthew and Clive's colleague, hadn't been there the night of the accident, so she couldn't see how any of them could have done it. She was a hundred percent sure that she could take Garcia off the list. But she left Brian there, just in case she needed to dig further into him.

That left her with only Clive and Mickey again. Both of them had been taken in and questioned, and yet, there were still so many unanswered questions.

At one point in the investigation, she'd even suspected them both, but contrasting timelines and lack of evidence had made her look the other way. Could they have actually been working together?

Sam backtracked and focused on Mickey because it was far more likely that she'd missed something about him than Clive. She thought back to their last conversation before he'd started yelling at her. What had he said when she asked about his father?

He'd been out with a woman. Actually, Mickey had called her a "dumb slut." But as far as she knew, Clive hadn't been dating anyone. Who was this woman? Did she know something she didn't?

Sadly, Sam had no name and no way of contacting this woman herself. And it wasn't like she could go digging and ask Mickey to spill some more details about her. Who else could she ask then? Would Matthew know about her? Would Maison?

Yes. Maison was her easiest way in! She knew everything that was going on at Gleam Enterprises!

Sam quickly dialed her number, happy to have found a stone yet unturned. When Maison answered, it was clear that she was outside by the ocean. "Hello?"

"Maison? It's me. Do you mind if I ask you a few questions about Clive again?"

"Sure, what do you want to know?" She was glad that she didn't have to explain herself, but she could tell that she'd caught her friend at a bad time.

"Where are you?"

"I'm at Dacey's house. I've got the day off." A pang of guilt went through her. Damn, she hated to disturb her while she was enjoying herself. "Sam? Are you still there?"

"You know what? Never mind. I'll just wait to talk to you tomorrow."

"No. Don't be silly. Why don't you come down here and we can talk?"

"Are you sure?" She felt terrible for if she ruined her day, but she also wanted to get to the bottom of this.

"Yes, I'm sure."

Because she couldn't help herself and because she knew she wouldn't be able to think of anything else but finding this mystery woman, she agreed. "Okay. I'm on my way."

* * *

When Sam arrived at Dacey's house, she was surprised to see several cars parked in the driveway. Thankfully, none of them was Hunter's but she worried that he might show up later. She had to be quick about this.

Instead of ringing the doorbell, Sam headed through the side of the house toward the beach where the music was coming from. Hutch was the first one to spot her and called her over. "What's up, stranger?" he asked as she came to stand beside him. He pulled her into a quick hug and Sam felt a pang of guilt hit her as she realized that she hadn't been spending that much time with her best friend.

Hutch looked down at her, a smile firmly in place. But then when he caught the emotion in her eyes, it faltered.

God, did he know already? Had Deacon called him? Deacon still hadn't called her back but maybe he'd already talked to them.

Sam braced herself. "Did you hear the news?"

Hutch nodded. "Yeah, I did. Deacon called me." *Dammit, so did that mean Hunter knew too?* "What the hell is going on?" he asked.

"That's what I'm trying to find out."

"Hey, Sam," Maison said as she approached them. "Are you okay?"

"Yeah, I'm just a little worried, that's all."

Maison nodded in understanding. "What did you want to ask me?"

Sam jumped straight into it, not wanting to waste any more time. "Do you know Clive's girlfriend?"

The other woman frowned. "No. I wasn't even aware that he was dating someone."

Huh. That was weird. According to Mickey, his father had been dating this mystery woman for at least a few months, so why then did no one know about it? While Maison was Matthew's assistant, she would still likely know these things if they were true. "He never mentioned he was seeing anyone to you?"

"No. Not at all. All this time, I thought he was still in love with his ex-wife."

"Do you know why they divorced?"

"I think she left him for another man."

"That's tragic," Hutch remarked.

"It is," she agreed. But that didn't tell her much about what she needed to know.

"I'm sorry," Maison said. "I didn't even realize he was with someone. He never mentioned her to me. Sorry I can't be of more help to you."

"Don't worry about it." But at least now she knew she was on the right track. What she was more worried about was Hunter. "Is Hunter coming here?"

"No. But that's because he probably hasn't checked his messages yet. Hey, wait a minute," Hutch suddenly called out. He pointed a finger behind her. "Look."

Sam turned, and her face fell when she saw Hunter and Owen walking toward them. *Uh oh.* She'd hoped to get this sorted out before seeing him again, but she should've known better. Her gaze immediately locked onto his, and even without words, she could see that he was pissed. "Oh shit," she mumbled.

As Owen joined Hutch and Maison, Hunter grabbed a hold of her arm. "Can we talk?"

"Ah, sure." She followed him away from the others. Inside of her stomach she felt like a snake was coiling and uncoiling.

"Why haven't you been answering my calls?"

"I'm sorry. I got a little distracted."

"Did you hear what happened?"

She nodded. "I was the one who the kid confessed to actually." Hunter's brows flew to his hairline. He obviously wasn't expecting that answer. "I'm really sorry." She really thought that everything was over with.

Hunter suddenly turned quiet. His gaze suddenly went to the ocean and his lips drew together in a line. "Today is just full of surprises, isn't it?"

What did that mean? She could tell that something was bothering him. She reached out and touched his back gently. "Is everything okay?"

Hunter shook his head and let out a long breath. "I saw Chrissy today."

"What? You mean—"

"Yeah, she came by Owen's school."

"Oh my God! What did he say when he saw her?"

"Nothing. Because he didn't see her."

Huh? "So what did she want?"

"She just walked to talk to me."

"Doesn't she have a phone?"

Hunter shrugged. "Chrissy has a weird way of doing things. Maybe she was just trying to flaunt off the fact that she's okay even after everything between us."

"Are *you* okay?" she asked him now. She hated seeing him like this. She really wished she could take some of his load off of him but it seemed like this entire thing didn't want to end.

"Yeah, I'll be fine. I think she just wanted to mess with me."

Sam wrapped her arms around him. "I'm just glad that you're okay." Hunter had already been through so much.

Hunter tightened his arms around her. "You don't have to worry about me."

He turned so that they were looking at his family on the other side of the beach. They all looked to be having a great time, laughing and smiling at something Owen was showing them. Despite the recent news, they looked better than she'd ever seen them together.

"Hey," Sam said, tilting her head up to look at Hunter. "I'm really sorry about not answering your calls earlier." She hated ignoring him and vowed to never do it again.

"It's okay." Hunter squeezed her tighter.

"We're going to figure this out," she whispered.

"It's not your fault, Sam. We'll find him or her sooner or later." Sooner, preferably. She was dying for this to be over. "But promise me one thing, Sam," Hunter said.

"What is it?"

"I don't want you investigating this. I know I asked this of you before and you didn't listen, but I mean it this time. No one knows what's going on and I don't want you to get hurt."

Sam wanted to argue but there was something in Hunter's eyes that stopped her. He looked sad. No, he wasn't just sad but *haunted*. Seeing his ex today had done more damage than she first realized. And although she felt like she might be onto something, Sam nodded.

Hunter pulled her in for a kiss, pouring every ounce of his love into her. Sam held on for the ride even as her head grew dizzy and her chest ached. "I love you, you know that?" he whispered against her lips.

"I love you, too."

Taking her hand, he led her back to the group. "I know it might be hard with everything that's going on, but let's just try to enjoy ourselves tonight, okay?"

"Okay." She saw no reason why they couldn't. It was better than wasting a single moment of this precious life they had.

TWENTY-SIX

WHEN SAM APPEARED ON CLIVE DAVENPORT'S doorstep the next day, she mentally went through her game plan one last time. While she'd promised Hunter that she wasn't going to investigate further, she just couldn't let this go. She hated lying and doing this behind his back, but Sam knew that if she wanted to bring him peace of mind, she had to go through with it. The Happa-Hewitts had already endured so much. There was no need to extend their suffering as they lived in fear of what might happen again if this person wasn't caught.

And technically, Sam could do whatever she wanted because Hunter couldn't fire her. She was just doing this on her own time. She had to tread carefully though. It wouldn't do any good if she got herself into trouble.

When she rang the doorbell, the man she came to see opened the door. Understandably, Clive looked baffled to see her standing there. "What are you doing here?" His tone was sharp and nasty.

Sam tried to make herself as friendly as possible. "I just want to ask you a few questions." There was a hint of apology in her tone, knowing that both she and the police had put him through the wringer.

"Well, I don't feel like answering them," he snapped.

She tried not to be offended. He was likely as tired of this as she was. "That's exactly what got us in this mess in the first place. Phillip Charms failed to tell the police everything and

Mickey paid the price for it. How many more people will have to be arrested before someone tells the truth around here? I just want to get to the bottom of this and then I'll leave you alone."

Conflict swam in Clive's eyes. Sam was tempted to push some more but realized that maybe she didn't have to when he asked, "What do you want to ask?"

"I'd like to know more about your girlfriend."

He turned closed in an instant. "My girlfriend? What does she have to do with anything?" He was clearly taken aback by the question, but Sam wondered if it was all an act. She'd already been fooled before so she was going to be wary of everything from now on.

"Well, I want to know why you haven't mentioned her to anyone. Mickey told me that you've been seeing her for a few months already and yet Maison had no clue you were dating anyone."

"I don't need to check in with her with my personal life."

"Maybe so, but I'd like to know more about her. Why don't you indulge me?"

At first he looked reluctant, but then he said, "Well, if you must know, she's not my girlfriend anymore. I broke up with her."

Sam couldn't hide her shock. Just a few days ago, Mickey had said he'd been out with her. "Is this recent?"

"Yes."

Hmm. Her curiosity was piqued now. Had that been the same day she'd come to see Mickey? "Can I ask why?"

Clive suddenly looked uncomfortable. He cleared his throat before speaking. "Things had taken a turn for the worse and I just felt like she was in the relationship for the wrong reasons."

Hmm. Interesting. "Do you mind sharing her name with

me? Maybe I could talk to her."

Clive shook his head. "I don't think that's a good idea."

"Why not?"

"I just don't think it'd be appropriate for you to seek her out since we've already broken up."

That wasn't how Sam saw it. Either Clive Davenport still had feelings for this woman and was extremely protective of her, or he was hiding something. Sam suspected it was the latter. "I'm sorry to say, but there's more at stake than what you consider appropriate or not."

For a moment, Clive looked worried. *Genuinely* worried. And that was when Sam knew that this was where she'd taken a wrong turn before.

God, how could she have not seen it before? Instead of jumping on it, she forced herself to keep her voice calm. "I can tell that you're hiding something from me, Mr. Davenport. It would benefit everyone, including you, if you told me what it is."

She could see that guilt was eating away at him little by little. Perhaps now it was becoming impossible to bear. Whatever he knew, whatever he'd done, it looked like it'd been torturing him for some time and Sam knew that when he came clean, it would change everything.

"Please," she begged. "Tell me what you know."

The loud sigh made his chest sound hollow. "Fine, I'll tell you."

Sam braced herself for the blow.

"I called her Mac but her real name is Chrissy McCartney,"

TWENTY-SEVEN

HUNTER WAS HAVING ANOTHER ONE OF THOSE DAYS where nothing seemed to be going right. Owen was having trouble napping because of a nightmare he'd had.

Although he knew there were no actual monsters under his bed, Hunter pretended to check anyway in the hopes of soothing his son. After repeatedly telling him it was just a dream and that everything was going to be okay, Owen finally relaxed.

Man, he loved this kid. No matter what he did, or what he said, Hunter would always be proud of his little boy. Owen was growing up so fast that he felt like the days were flying by him. If he blinked, maybe he'd miss it. One day Owen would grow up and no longer need him. So he'd cherish every moment he had with him, especially moments like this when he wouldn't let go.

He was paying for it now though. His brain felt like it had been put through the washing machine. Which actually reminded him that he'd forgotten to do the laundry last night. *Again.* His body also felt like he'd been through the wars, experiencing aches and pains in places he had no reason to be. He couldn't even remember the last time he'd worked out. It had to be before he started to work at Gleam. He just hadn't had the time recently, but it was time to stop with the excuses and get back into the groove. *Yes. He would do that*, he decided. *Today.* He couldn't very well keep up with Owen when he wasn't in shape himself. But first, he needed some coffee.

He made the brew before opening one of the cupboards, intending to take down a coffee mug. What he pulled down instead was a wine glass. Hunter chuckled to himself. Okay, so maybe it *was* going to be one of those days.

Replacing it, he grabbed what he really wanted and then poured himself a cup of hot coffee. After consuming the heavenly nectar, he made sure Hutch was okay with watching Owen while he made his way to the gym.

Once there, he went through his regular workout. He started with a quick warm-up to prepare his muscles for the torture he was going to put himself through, but he only made it through twenty minutes on the treadmill when his phone rang. "Hello?" He'd answered without checking, assuming it was either Sam or one of his siblings. But he hadn't expected *her.*

"Hunter?"

He froze at the sound of his name and hit the ground hard. Sprawled out on the floor and in excruciating pain, Hunter stared at the phone on the floor next to him. *Chrissy? What the hell was she doing calling him?*

"Hey, you okay, man?" someone asked as they moved to him to help but Hunter paid him no mind as he picked up the phone again and growled, "What do you want?"

"Hunter, please." Chrissy's voice was shaky and emotional. "I need to see you." He reared back from the emotion in her voice. *What the hell, was she crying?*

Quickly, Hunter collected his things and grabbed his bag, moving to a more private area. "What's wrong?" he asked, hating himself as he did so. He vowed to himself that he wouldn't fall for her lies again.

"Everything." He could hear Chrissy's sobs as they grew

louder. "Everything is *terrible*."

Now what could be so terrible in her perfect little life? She had it so much better than he did. What could upset her so much? Had her barista boyfriend dumped her? Surprisingly, Chrissy changed the subject. "Will you let me see Owen? I think that would make me feel better."

Alarm bells started clanging in his head. His immediate reaction was to say no but then he thought of what Owen would want. Did he still miss her? And if he did, could he do that to him? Could he really stop his mother from trying to see her own child?

"Why do you want to see him?" he heard himself ask. *Wait. He wasn't actually considering this, was he?* Up until this moment, Chrissy had never shown an interest in seeing Owen again. And that had been totally fine with him. If he had it his way, he would never let his kid meet his traitorous mother again. But what if Owen grew up hating him because he'd selfishly kept him away from Chrissy because of his own hurt? Hunter couldn't do that to him.

"Owen misses you," he heard himself say. "Sometimes he even cries for you."

Chrissy sobbed even harder. "Can I see him?" she asked. "Right now?"

"He's not with me right now."

"Where is he?"

"He's at home. Hutch is watching him. I'm leaving the gym right now."

"Can I see *you* then?"

"Me? Ah, I don't know if that's a good idea." *What would she want with him?*

"Come on, Hunt. I just want to talk. I want to know how Owen is doing. Maybe we can discuss a way for me to come see him?" She'd stopped crying and her voice sounded . . . hopeful.

"I don't know." He wasn't sure how he felt about all of this actually.

"Please?"

A vision of Owen popped into his mind then. And then he thought about how he'd been last night, scared out of his wits because of the nightmares he'd had. *Protect him.* He'd vowed to do that ever since the day he was born. But was it his mother that he had to protect Owen from? Hunter sighed heavily. He had no idea what to do. "Okay," he said before he could change his mind. "Where do you want to meet?"

"There's a park on Rose Boulevard. Can we meet there?"

That wasn't a great distance from where he was now. "Okay, I'll be there in fifteen."

"Great. I'll see you there."

He hung up without saying goodbye. He still couldn't believe he was going to do this. As he slid into his car, he wondered if he'd come to regret this later. Sighing, Hunter pulled out onto the road. "Well, there's only one way to find out."

Sam blinked. And then she had to blink again. "Wait. *Chrissy?* Isn't that—"

Clive nodded, looking ashamed.

What the hell? "No. No, it can't be." That couldn't be possible. Why the hell would he hook up with Hunter's *ex-wife?* Suddenly the pieces were clicking together in her mind. *"How could you?"*

"I didn't know she was his ex!"

"Oh, *bullshit!* You can't expect me to believe that!"

"No! Seriously! We met at a dinner party a few months back. I'll admit, I was a little surprised that she was interested in me. She's so beautiful and so *young."*

"And that didn't throw you off?"

"It did at first. But after that I didn't care. A lot of women are interested in me because of the money I have. I liked her enough that I didn't mind."

"You didn't care that she was the ex-wife of your business partner's son?" Sam couldn't believe any of this!

"I told you, I didn't know she was. When I found out, that's when I broke up with her."

Sam gritted her teeth. How could she believe that? Clive and Matthew had been business partners for years. Hadn't he met Chrissy while she'd been married to Hunter? But then she remembered how the Happa-Hewitts hadn't gotten along. They'd go months without speaking to each other. It was entirely possible that they hadn't crossed paths at all. Hell, she herself hadn't spent much time with Hunter even though she was best friends with his brother. But could it really be possible? Could Clive really not have known what he was getting himself into? "What's the real reason why you broke up with her?" she asked.

Clive pursed his lips together. "I already told you. I found out about her connection to Hunter. And then I thought that maybe she might be the one who had tried to have Matthew killed."

God, she really couldn't believe this. It was so fucked up. Ripping her phone from her pocket, Sam quickly called Hunter. Was that why Chrissy had suddenly shown up out of the blue again? Because Clive had decided that he was done with her?

"How did you find out about her past with Hunter?"

"From Mickey. While I was inside with Matthew that night, he was on his way out. He told me that Chrissy had come back. I remember that she'd used my car that day to run a few errands."

"So Mickey took the car after that."

"Yes."

Holy shit. That was why she wasn't able to figure it out! It was because she was missing a big piece of the puzzle! She hadn't anticipated that someone else other that Clive and Mickey had been there that night!

"Did he say how long she'd been outside alone?"

"I don't know exactly but I assume a while." Long enough that she probably had time to mess with the brakes.

Sam cursed and pulled the phone from her ear. "Why the hell isn't he picking up?" Hunter always answered the phone for her. *Oh God, what if something had happened to him?* Dread pierced through her chest like a lance. "I have to go," she said quickly. "Chrissy might be with Hunter right now."

Before she could leave, Clive grabbed a hold of her arm. His eyes were filled with worry and apology. "I'm sorry. I should've told someone sooner and now—"

Sam pulled free. "There's no time. I have to go." If she didn't get to Hunter in time, he might be the next Happa-Hewitt that Chrissy would target.

TWENTY-EIGHT

THE PARK WAS EMPTY WHEN HE ARRIVED AND THIS suited Hunter just fine. He had no idea how this was going to go down, but he figured that the less people here to witness them arguing, the better.

He still wasn't sure what he was doing here. Had Chrissy's tears really weakened him that much that he'd actually agreed to meet her? *God, what the hell was wrong with him?* He suddenly regretted his decision to come here. He wanted to do the right thing for his son, but now he wondered if he was making another mistake. Once again, he was allowing her to play him for a fool. Hunter was just about to get up to head back to his car when the sound of clicking heels froze him in place.

Even though it wasn't the most practical choice of shoe wear to wear to the park, Chrissy never went anywhere without her heels. She was the kind of person who valued vanity above all. "Hello, Hunter," she said when she reached him.

For a moment, Hunter took a moment to take her in. His ex-wife looked regal in a form-fitting pencil skirt and collared blouse. Her fine hair was pinned back, showing off the soft angles of her face. Big round sunglasses shielded her eyes from him. She looked pretty good for someone who'd just been crying oceans on the phone with him. Again, he wondered if it'd been all an act. At this point, he knew Chrissy wouldn't be above it.

Hunter stood there, unsure if he should pull her into a hug or shake her hand. Instead, he settled for standing there like an idiot. "Hi."

"Hi. Can we sit down?"

"Actually, I'll stand." He didn't plan on staying for very long anyway. He just wanted to hear what she wanted to say about Owen and then he was going to leave.

"Fine. Suit yourself." Chrissy lowered herself to the bench, immediately crossing her legs in that feminine way that always worked in getting him to look at them.

This time, however, Hunter kept his gaze on her face, studying it for her intentions. "So you said you wanted to set up a way to see Owen?" he prompted.

"Yes. I miss him. I think it'd be nice of him to see me again. What do you think?"

"Yes," he agreed. "I'm sure he'd like that." *He* wouldn't. But what he wanted didn't factor into any of this.

His phone rang suddenly and Hunter pulled it from his pocket. Sam's name flashed on the caller ID but he knew better than to take her call in front of Chrissy. His ex had always been the jealous type, requiring his full attention and he'd rather not have to put Sam through all that. So he quickly hit Ignore and shoved his phone back into his pocket.

"Do you think he'd be interested in staying with me for a few days?" Chrissy asked, bringing his attention back to their conversation.

"I think that's a bit soon, don't you think?" Just a few days ago, she had no interest in seeing Owen.

"Why? I mean it's not like I'm a stranger to him. I'm his *mother*."

"You are," he agreed. "But he hasn't seen you in months." And he wasn't just about to hand Owen over to her like he was an object.

"Oh, he'll be fine. I'll take good care of him."

"No." His voice was firm and authoritative. When it came to the safety and well-being of his son, there was no leniency. "What you're going to do is try talking to him first. You know, spend a couple of hours with him or something. And then if he decides he likes you, we can work up to more."

Chrissy rose to her feet again. "Would *you* be there?" A hopeful look lit her eyes and it reminded him a lot of the old times they used to share together.

"Of course." He wasn't going to leave him out of his sight while she was with him. He wasn't *that* stupid.

His phone rang again but he didn't bother pulling it out. *Dammit, Sam. Not now.*

With a smile, Chrissy closed the distance between them. "Aww. You're upset." She reached out, intending to touch his face but Hunter grabbed a hold of her hand, stopping her before she could do it.

"Chrissy," he warned. "This is strictly going to be about Owen." He had no plans to rekindle what they once had. That was over and done with. And this meeting was strictly, and *only*, for their son.

Chrissy pouted. "Oh, don't be like that. We used to be good together. Don't you remember?"

"Those days are long gone." Besides, he had someone else now. Someone he loved very much. Sam was everything Hunter wanted and needed and he wanted nothing more than her.

"You're thinking about her, aren't you?"

Hunter frowned. "What?"

"That woman you've been seeing. The private investigator. She's the one who's calling you, right?"

Hunter felt his blood run cold. *How the hell did she know about Sam?* He hadn't mentioned her. Not once.

"What do you know about Sam?" His words had come out sharp and slicing. He was going to protect Sam at all costs.

But Chrissy just gave him a lizard smile. Her next words chilled him to the bone. "I know more about her than you can ever imagine . . ."

Sam had always been pretty good at cussing but now she was inventing curse words that she'd never heard in her entire life. *Where the fuck was Hunter? Why wasn't he answering any of her calls? Was something wrong?*

She made a quick call to Deacon, requesting for back-up because she honestly didn't know what she was going to find when she found Hunter. Plus, she needed him to help her track him down. "Wait, wait," her friend said now as she hastily filled him in on what she'd discovered. "Let me get this straight. Are you telling me that Clive was seeing Hunter's ex-wife all this time and no one knew about it?"

"Yes. I know it sounds crazy but that was the piece of the puzzle that we missed! I remember that his ex-wife was always asking if Hunter was going to take his father's place at Gleam Enterprises, so we know that she was interested. Problem was, Hunter never wanted to follow in his father's footsteps."

"Do you think that's why they got a divorce?"

Holy shit. Was that the reason? She knew Chrissy had cheated on him, but maybe that had just been a cover-up for the real reason why she left him. "Oh God, Hunter doesn't even know . . ." Her heart broke for him.

"So Chrissy married Hunter," Deacon continued, "think-ing it was her way of getting to the family's company. But Hunter didn't end up going into it."

"That's right."

"So she divorced him and started dating Clive Davenport instead?"

"Right again." This woman was so desperate to find a way into the company that she'd been willing to do anything for it.

"How does that explain the brakes then?"

"Clive just told me she'd used his car earlier that day to run errands. And I remember Hunter saying that his ex-wife knows a lot about cars since her father owned a garage when she was little. She would know how to tamper with the brakes without making it seem like something was wrong with them."

"She knew how to do that all by herself?" Deacon sounded skeptical.

"Hey, women are just as capable as men," Sam chided. "Plus, we don't know what time she returned from running her errands. For all we know, she could've been out there for an hour or more before Mickey came out."

"What about the stain on the car?"

"We all thought it had been Mickey who'd done it, but I think that was Chrissy too. That was her second mistake, leaving something like that behind."

"Okay, I got it," Deacon said suddenly. "Hunter is in a park on Rose Boulevard. Do you know it?"

"Yeah. Meet you there."

"Don't go in without me, okay? We don't know if she's armed or something." Dread filled her as she pictured Hunter being held at gunpoint. *Oh God, she had to hurry!* Sam was already on the move, turning back onto the road. "I mean it, Sam," Deacon said sternly.

"Okay! I promise I won't!"

"But before you go, tell me one more thing: what was her first mistake?"

"Huh?"

"You said that the stain was her second mistake. What was the first?"

Sam stepped hard on the gas. Her words came out as a snarl. "Her first mistake was messing with the Happa-Hewitts and thinking she could get away with it."

TWENTY-NINE

"**A**NSWER THE QUESTION!" HUNTER SHOUTED. HE'D always had a high tolerance for Chrissy's bullshit but that was only when it came to himself. When she started on other people, like his family or in this case, Sam, he wouldn't tolerate it. *At all.*

Chrissy smiled evilly. "You're protective of her. How fascinating."

What was fascinating was the fact that she found this to be amusing. He had no idea what was going on but he was beginning to think that maybe she hadn't called him out here because she wanted to discuss Owen. What did she really want then? Challenge flashed in her bright eyes as he put his guard up. "What do you want?" he asked finally. He didn't want to be lied to anymore. And he was sick and tired of playing her games.

"I want you," she purred. Her soft voice grated like nails on a chalkboard. "I want what we had before."

Hunter shook his head. "Sorry, but that's never going to happen."

"Why? Is it because of this Sam lady?"

"No, it's because you cheated on me with some scumbag!"

Chrissy rolled her eyes. "He was nothing. *You're* the one that I want. Come on, let's be together again." She reached for him suddenly and Hunter couldn't get away quick enough. Her hand came down on his neck, bringing him down toward her.

"*Let go!*" he thundered, prying her fingers off one by one

until her grip loosened and he broke free. "How many times do I have to tell you? It's *never* going to happen. *What's done is done!*"

At his angry outburst, Chrissy's eyes went wide before narrowing in slits.

God, how did he allow himself to get into this mess again? How could he ever think that Chrissy actually missed her son when she didn't have a heart to begin with? He had to stop trying to see the good in people when there clearly wasn't any.

He was still trying to devise a way out of this situation when Sam came running around the corner. *"Hunter! Get away from her!"* she screamed.

Hunter couldn't hide his surprise. "Sam?" *What the hell was she doing here?*

But her gaze wasn't on him. It was focused on Chrissy. His ex-wife turned, surprised to see Deacon also coming around the corner, gun raised and ready to shoot. "What's all this?"

Yeah. He'd like to know the same thing.

"Oh, shut up," Sam snapped. "Stop pretending already. We already know you were behind it all."

"What are you talking about?" Chrissy asked.

"Sam?" he called out, prompting her to explain. "What's going on?" *Why the hell were they here?*

"She's the one," she said. "She's the one who tried to kill your father."

What? How could that be?

"What are you talking about?" Chrissy sneered. "You don't have anything on me. You've just walked into a martial dispute. That's all."

"You're not married anymore, so cut the shit." Sam came around to him while Deacon stayed beside Chrissy, weapon still raised.

"I'm sorry," she told him. "I tried calling you but you weren't picking up."

Oh God. That was what this was all about? She'd been trying to warn him! Hunter pulled her into him, hugging her hard. He felt terrible now for ignoring her calls. "It's okay. Just fill me in on what's going on." Apparently, a lot had happened that he didn't know yet.

"I hate to be the one to tell you but after you two divorced, she started seeing Clive." He glanced at Chrissy, trying to gage her reaction but she wasn't giving anything away. "She was hoping that would be her way into the company when you didn't show an interest in taking your father's place at Gleam. After she left you, she sought out other means to get what she wanted. But she got impatient and needed to get your father out of the picture so that Clive would become the CEO."

"But Matthew didn't die in the accident and she wasn't expecting you to take his place," Deacon finished for her. "Clive found out about her plans and dumped her. Which is why she's here talking with you, trying to get you to take her back."

What the hell? How could all of this happen? Had he just been a pawn in her game all this time? He turned to Chrissy again. "Is this true?" *Had he been played all along?*

"Come on, Chrissy," Sam snarled. "Just admit it. The person who tampered with the brakes would've needed uninterrupted time, which Mickey wouldn't have had. And they would've needed to know a lot about cars, which you do, having worked in your father's garage all your life."

Hunter felt like he'd been punched in the gut as Sam's words sunk in. Even worse was the fear he saw now in Chrissy's eyes. Everything she was being accused of was true. *It had been her the whole time!*

Motherfucker!

Hunter wasn't sure if he should be relieved that they'd finally caught the person who'd tried to hurt them or be angry for not realizing all this before the people he loved were hurt. He felt foolish for not realizing it earlier.

Chrissy's mean snake-like smile made his stomach curl. "It must feel good to have figured it all out, huh? And they say women aren't as smart as men." Chrissy turned to him, eyes sharp. "It's your fault, you know. I only decided to do it because you refused to take over."

No. He hadn't asked for this. He hadn't—

"Don't listen to her," Sam snapped. She grabbed a hold of him, forcing him to look at her in the eyes. "You didn't do anything wrong."

He had. His father had come to him to ask him to take his place at Gleam and he'd said no. He should've just agreed. He should've said yes way before any of this could happen. It would've prevented all this from happening. But if he'd done that he never would have met Sam and he probably wouldn't be as happy as he was now.

Sam shook him, pulling him back from his thoughts. "Hunter, are you listening to me? Do you understand? You did nothing wrong."

Hunter gave a slow nod. "Yes. I understand."

She embraced him then and he caught the glittering of tears in her eyes. He'd never seen Sam this shaken up before and all he could do was hold on and breathe her scent in. He was so happy to have her in his life.

When he looked back up, it was to see Deacon putting his gun away and slapping out a pair of handcuffs. He secured them around Chrissy's wrists and began to take her away. Her confession was going to finally put this all to rest.

Hunter couldn't have been happier.

Sam took in Hunter's broad shoulders and emotionless eyes and wished there was something else she could do to comfort him. She knew she'd just dropped a bomb on him but she was also glad that he was safe. "Hey, are you okay?"

"I'm fine. Are you?"

"I'm good." Now that she knew Chrissy was being taken care of, she had nothing to be worried about. She could finally relax. On her way here though, she was pretty sure she'd experienced a mild heart attack with the way her heart was thumping with fear in her chest. Thankfully, they'd arrived before anything could happen to Hunter.

"You did it." Hunter smiled down at her proudly. "You figured it all out."

"I'm just relieved I got here in time." She'd been *so* terrified for him.

"I'm fine," he assured her. "Everything is fine now."

"What would you have done if I hadn't shown up? Would you have gotten back with her?" She hated that she asked, but she genuinely wanted to know.

Hunter snorted. "No way. That part of my life has passed." He shot her a lopsided smile that turned her insides to goo. "Besides, my sexy girlfriend would probably get jealous."

Sam made a face. "I'm not jealous."

"Oh, I wasn't talking about you," Hunter drawled.

She swatted his arm and Hunter laughed as he pulled her into his arms. "I'm just kidding. You're the only woman I want."

"Better be," she muttered. "So what do you think your father will say when he learns of what really happened that night?"

"I don't know. He'll probably be pissed at me and tell me I'm an idiot for not listening to him."

"Really?"

Hunter shrugged. "I think he might be relieved actually. I think he just wants this whole thing to be over with."

"It *is* over now, so you can all relax. I think he'll probably be surprised."

"Oh yeah. But at least he won't have to face Clive and feel awkward about it."

Huh? "Won't face each other? That's a little hard to do when they're both partners in the same business together."

Hunter turned, locking his dark eyes on her. "Matthew isn't coming back to work for Gleam actually," he told her. "He's retiring."

"What?" *How did she not know this?*

"Yeah. He said it would be hard for him to return and pick up where he left off." Guess that made sense. "Plus, it's about time," Hunter continued. "He wants to spend his days relaxing now."

"What about you?" she asked. "Are you going to stay on?"

Hunter was quick to nod. "I know I didn't want the job at first, but now, I can't see myself leaving. It's funny how your dreams change like that."

Sam grinned and leaned further into his arms. "Yeah. I know all about that." She had never planned to become a private investigator but now she couldn't see herself as anything else.

Sam rose up on her tiptoes and placed her mouth on his. She was so proud of this man. "You're going to do a great job," she whispered. Just like he'd done a wonderful job of raising Owen, he was going to do the same with Gleam Enterprises.

"Thanks, but I couldn't have done it without you."

Tightening her arms around him, Sam kissed him again, pouring all her love into it. After today, she knew that her life was going to change. Whereas before she had lived her life to carry out her passion, now she was living to spend more time with her family and friends.

From all this, she learned that there was nothing more important than family and she vowed to never again take them for granted. Because although there were times when you didn't get along, when times got tough, they would be the only ones there for you.

"Let's go home," she whispered when they pulled apart.

With a smile, Hunter took her hand and, together, they walked away from one chapter of their lives into—hopefully—a better one.

THIRTY

"I NOW PRONOUNCE YOU HUSBAND AND WIFE."

Hunter let out a long wolf whistle as Hutch and Maison embraced and fell into a sultry lip-lock. It was funny how he went from attending no weddings at all to being present in two this year. And it was even stranger to think that his little brother was now a married man.

As the bride and groom took each other's hand, they walked down the aisle for the first time as husband and wife. Hunter did his best to not get too emotional. He knew for a fact that crying like a baby wasn't a good look for him, but he never thought he'd get a chance to see this moment. He'd always assumed that Hutch would be overseas somewhere, stupidly risking his life, not back here in Moonrise Beach where they'd all grown up together.

His brother had suffered alone and in silence instead of seeking comfort from his family and Hunter still felt guilty about that, but things had finally changed for them. When their father had gotten into the accident, he and his siblings had come together to take care of him, displaying a love he thought long disappeared when their mother had died.

Matthew came to stand beside him. "So what did you think of it?" Hunter asked as they watched Hutch and Maison fondly.

"I thought it was beautiful. I only wish your mother was here to see it."

Surprised by the words, Hunter turned to his father. He had to admit, he looked pretty good all dressed up like that.

He looked even better because there was color in his face. He seemed to be fully recovered from his accident. "Yeah," he agreed on a whisper. "That would've been nice." But he wouldn't dwell on that now when they had so much to be thankful for.

That was when Dacey approached them, her eyes sparkling with happiness. "What are you two talking about? It's Hutch's wedding day! We're supposed to be happy."

"We *are* happy," he shot back as he pulled her into his arms. He then grinned over his sister's shoulder at Greyson, who nodded in return. "You look beautiful, by the way."

"Thanks. Where's Sam?"

"I'm right here." They all spun around to find Sam standing behind them. Owen was glued at her side, looking perfectly content as she held his hand.

Sam looked absolutely stunning in her dress. It showed of all her curves, and more importantly, her tattoos, so that she looked just as radiant as the bride. She walked toward them and Hunter bent to pick up Owen. "So now that Hutch is married, do you think he's going to move in with Maison?"

"I don't know," Matthew said. "He never mentioned anything about it." While living with his brother and father hadn't been what he'd wanted initially, Hunter was going to miss having everyone all under one roof.

Sam spoke up then, drawing in everyone's eyes. She addressed Matthew in a respectful voice. "Mr. Hewitt, I just want to say that I'm very sorry for everything that happened. I'm sorry we didn't figure out what happened earlier."

His father grinned at her. "Don't worry about any of that, Sam. I should be the one thanking you for what you've done for my family. For protecting Hunter the way you have."

Sam's cheeks reddened. "I was just doing my job."

"You've done a hell of a lot better than anyone else. Do you want to come have dinner with us next Friday?"

She looked surprised by the offer. Hell, he was too. His father usually didn't invite anyone to their Friday family dinners. "Really?" She nodded. "I'd love to."

"Just a warning though," he said before she could get too excited. "It's usually pretty crazy." Having all the Happa-Hewitts together always made for a rowdy time.

Sam shot him a gamine grin. "Don't worry. I think I'm used to it."

"Then please, come join my family."

EPILOGUE

D EACON HATED DELAYS. EVEN MORE, HE HATED BEING wrong. Twice now he'd mistakenly believed that two innocent people had been involved in committing a crime. And to make matters worse, his errors in judgment had been splattered over every major headline in the news. Even though they'd finally gotten the right person behind the accident, Deacon wasn't sure he could save his reputation.

"How long are you going to sit there and stare at your computer screen?" Glancing up, he caught sight of Juliana standing over him. His friend was as smart as she was beautiful, and she was currently giving him the stink eye.

"Ah." He didn't even realize that he was doing that.

Her hand came over his shoulder and gave it a squeeze. "Why don't you head on home? It might be good to get some rest. You've been working yourself to the bone."

He had to if he wanted to avoid making more mistakes. Although he didn't necessarily strive for perfection, he wanted to be damn close to it.

Juliana's face appeared beside his. "Go home," she whispered. "People will forget what happened."

Not likely. Clive Davenport was a high-profile guy and when you threw in Gleam Enterprises, one of the biggest companies in the world, he doubted people would forget that easily. He should consider himself lucky that he hadn't been fired from his job.

Juliana straightened and made her way around his desk.

"Fine. Suit yourself. But you're being too hard on yourself. I think both the Happa-Hewitts and Sam would be happy with what you've done for them."

Deacon couldn't deny that they were good people and he'd been more than happy to help them. He just wished that they hadn't had to go through so many loops to find out what had actually happened that night.

When Sam had brought that Charms kid in, he knew he'd fucked up somewhere. And that was unacceptable. How could he consider himself to be the best on the force if he kept making stupid mistakes like that?

In this line of business, he was well aware that sometimes you won and sometimes you learned. Deacon recently learned that he had to be more cautious before he acted. So from now on, there would be no more partying and no more assing around. He really had to focus if he wanted to regain what respect he had in his field.

After Juliana left to go home, Deacon shut down his computer and grabbed his things to leave. Although he was tired, he knew he wouldn't get a wink of sleep tonight. Regardless, tomorrow morning he would come in early again with the hopes of working hard and atoning for his mistakes.

DRIVE ME WILD

Moonrise Beach series, Book Four

After escaping an emotionally abusive relationship, Olivia Edwards returns to her hometown of Moonrise Beach for refuge. But no matter how much time has passed, her rebellious past continues to haunt her. Everyone remembers her as a troublemaking wild child and wishes for her to leave, but Olivia is set on walking the straight and narrow while making Moonrise Beach her forever home.

Deacon Thorpe of the Moonrise Beach Police Department won't make it easy for her though. After his reputation has been tarnished, he has made a new rule for himself—no more women. Restricting himself means that there won't be any more trouble under his watch.

But when Olivia is caught committing a foolish crime, Deacon has no choice but to punish her. In doing so, he realizes that the stories about her may not all be true. Can Deacon protect his heart from Olivia's wild ways? Or will she teach him that there is no such thing as rules when it comes to love?

Be notified when new titles are released by subscribing to my newsletter at www.anajolene.com

RESURRECTION

Glory MC series, Book Four

When the president of the club goes missing, Beck Caulder, one of Glory MC's sergeant at arms, is the one to strap on his anti-radiation gear and go in search for him. The problem is, Knuckle has a hit on him, which means Beck won't be the only one on the lookout.

When Beck discovers that the president is hiding in Westborough, the most dangerous place in Ward Four, he has no choice but to run headlong into Slasher territory. There, he encounters Devine Blaise, the raven-haired beauty, covered in leather and tattoos. With her killer bod and equally killer instincts, Devine quickly becomes Beck's dream woman. Too bad she's also the mercenary hired to take out his club's president.

Equally matched in determination and skill, the chase soon becomes a battle of the most deadly as Beck and Devine try to take each other out. This should be easy for the club's sergeant at arms, but resisting the killer becomes the hardest battle he's ever fought—and the only one Beck fears he can't win.

Be notified when new titles are released by subscribing to my newsletter at www.anajolene.com

ACKNOWLEDGMENTS

MORE THAN THIS was definitely one of the biggest challenges of my writing career so far. Not only did it round out the Happa-Hewitt story arc, but it also included my first mystery subplot. If I knew how hard it was going to be then I wouldn't have done it, but I'm still glad that I challenged and pushed myself out of my comfort zone.

Many thanks go out to my team of experts. Without you, Karen and Judy, I wouldn't be able to share my books with the world. Thank you Stacey for your amazing work. You're the only one who I have kept through this entire journey and I hope to keep you on my side for more adventures.

Thank you Ariel for providing me with everlasting support. I hope we can be together forever. And thank you to my parents for being there and for letting me live out my dreams.

And lastly, to the fans and bloggers who read my books, you have no idea how precious you are to me. Thank you *so* much! I hope you can continue to support me through this journey.

ABOUT THE AUTHOR

Ana Jolene is the author of the Glory MC series, a New Adult Dystopian and the Contemporary Romance series, Moonrise Beach.

Growing up as a rebellious kid didn't allow for much reading time. It wasn't until Ana was in university that she found her passion for books and has since then devoured every book placed before her. Ana holds a B.A. in Psychology and has worked in both IT and Administration. But she's had the most fun in the bookish world, working as a reviewer, columnist, and assistant to multiple sites and best-selling authors.

Ana currently lives in Toronto with her family and an extremely lazy Shih Tzu whom she adores. To learn more about Ana and her books, please visit her website www.anajolene.com and subscribe to the newsletter to be notified of the hottest new releases and giveaways!

Connect with Ana:

Twitter: @ anajoleneauthor

Facebook: www.facebook.com/anajoleneauthor

Instagram: www.instagram.com/anajoleneauthor

Website: www.anajolene.com

OTHER TITLES BY ANA JOLENE

Glory MC series
Glory
Origin
Nirvana
Resurrection (Coming Soon)

Moonrise Beach series
Close To You
Sweet As Sin
More Than This
Drive Me Wild (Coming Soon)

www.ingramcontent.com/pod-product-compliance
Lightning Source LLC
Chambersburg PA
CBHW050419260626
47156CB00003B/1074